MORE THAN YOU SAY

BACKSTAGE BOOK TWO

REBECCA STONE

STARR STREET PUBLISHING

All rights reserved. No part of this book may be reproduced in any form or by any electronic means, including information storage and retrieval systems, without permission in writing from the author, except by a reviewer who may quote brief passages in review.

This is a work of fiction. Any resemblance to actual persons, living or dead, events, or locales is entirely coincidental. Any trademarks, service marks, product names, or named features are assumed to be the property of their respective owners, and are used only for reference. There is
no implied endorsement if any of these terms are used.

Copyright © 2020 by Rebecca Stone
All rights reserved.
Cover design by Rebecca Stone
ISBN

1

Anthony stood in a corner, watching the crowd decked out in New Year's hats and tiaras. The metallic taste of the Coke in his glass burned so good.

But not as good as the whiskey he wished it was.

The small New York City apartment was crowded, people dressed to the nines and ready to ring in a new year. A new year filled with hopes that would eventually be dashed. Resolutions that would never come to fruition. A new year with broken hearts and missed opportunities. Anthony sighed, taking another sip. The party doubled as a housewarming for his cousin and bandmate Gideon and his fiancée Ella. Gideon was in the living room while he talked to anyone who would listen about how their band, Eternal Youths, was starting to record their second album.

"Hey, Ant. You doing okay?" Ella's soft voice came up next to him, a gentle hand resting on his shoulder. He swallowed before turning to the woman who was a spitting image of her best friend, the woman he'd lost.

"Yep. Peachy. Nice digs you guys got." He sipped his soda, trying to push the image of Julie Milligan from his mind. Anthony knew she'd taken off to travel the world back in September, but he'd deleted all his social media, and Gideon knew better than to talk about Julie in front of Anthony. Especially after the way she'd ripped his heart out after they'd had the most amazing night together.

"Thanks, it helps Gideon's such a neat freak." Ella laughed, surveying the room. "I know I'm not supposed to talk about it but I know this is a romantic holiday. So how are you really holding up?" Ell tipped her head, brow furrowed.

Anthony barked out a laugh. "Please, Ella. I'm fine. I hope Julie finds what she deserves. Excuse me, I think I see my friend."

He pushed past Ella, ignoring her shocked look.

He knew it was rude, but he couldn't take it anymore. Couldn't take the pity, the questions, the way Ella's blonde hair reflected light like Julie's did. The way Ella's green eyes should've been Julie's blue. The way Julie should've been there.

Moving through the kitchen, he saw his dad Tom, the band's manager, laughing beside an older woman who radiated happiness. Anthony hadn't seen his dad this happy since... since Anthony was a kid and his mom was still around. Before she'd left them both without so much as a goodbye. Anthony felt the anger rising. He could justify it — the love of his life had destroyed him, the message he'd sent to his mom after tracking her down had gone unanswered, his cousin was getting married — but knew he shouldn't. He remembered back when he drank and did drugs, how he could mask the anger and depression for a time. But it always came back.

After the drunk car accident he was in last fall and the rehab stint he did the past spring, he knew the emotions he felt sober would always outweigh the consequences of hiding them drunk or high. Not that it wasn't hard, but it was manageable.

He pushed his way through the kitchen, stopping in the hallway by the bathroom. It was quieter here; it was closing in on midnight so most of the partygoers were finding their way to the living room or kitchen where there was a view of the famed ball drop on the TV. Now six months sober, Anthony realized he preferred being alone to being in a crowd. He didn't mind the ebb and flow of moving with others, learning how and when to move amongst everyone else in their own dance, but there was something about the space of silence he'd found a home in.

"I've always hated crowds."

Anthony turned to the speaker, a woman, red curls framing a freckled face. She smiled at him, a small gap between her front teeth. "Hi, I'm Ruby."

"Anthony. I don't mind crowds but I prefer no crowds." He gave her a small smile before sipping his dwindling drink. Eyeing the strappy heels on Ruby's feet, following the line of her long legs to the black dress that hugged her slender figure and ample chest.

She was so far from Julie.

Anthony heard the countdown begin in the other room, the air vibrating with the chorus of numbers and excited laughter. He pounded his soda. He hadn't been with someone since that fateful night with Julie, not since he'd woken beside her as if in a dream only to have her say it'd been a mistake.

If there was ever a time to try and move on, a cute redhead at a dry New Year's party would be a good start.

2

The province of Treviso was as quaint as Julie had expected, the Italian countryside outside of Venice boasting cobblestone streets, blue-green canals with swimming ducks, and flowered balconies attached to old stone buildings. The excited, lilting Italian language could be heard through the air, the rich scent of espresso weaving its way through the words.

Julie stopped at a bus marker, the vehicle rattling down the street towards her. She checked her map before climbing aboard. She'd gotten comfortable with the various bus maps in Europe, but that was more so because they'd taught her a lot about letting go of control. Sometimes she got on the wrong one, like in Dublin when trying to get to Glasnevin

Cemetery. Or she rode past her stop, like in London when she was trying to get to the secret swimming pond in Hampstead Heath. By the time she'd gotten to France, she'd decided to stick with the metro system. But that had been an issue all in itself, so she realized above ground she could at least walk everywhere.

She'd left New York, left her job, back in September to try and find something more. After confronting the loss of her sister ten years ago in an accident she hadn't caused but was a driver in, Julie had realized the life she'd built as a lawyer was more to make her parents happy than for her. She sighed, leaning her head against the cold bus window, watching the passing buildings on her way back to the Treviso airport. She'd given each country a mission — strength, self-care, compassion, to name a few — and had cut romantic relationships out of her life for the duration of her travels. Ireland, England, France, the Netherlands, Germany, Italy. Onto India, Nepal, Thailand, Malaysia. Then home.

Whatever home was.

The bus pulled in front of the tiny airport that was the hub for Venice. Julie had left her hostel in Venice that morning, terrified she'd mess up the public transport and miss her flight. She hadn't — had actually gotten there hours before they would start boarding — and had decided to take a short trip into town.

Grabbing her backpack, she made her way into the airport and scanned for a spot. The upstairs held a little cafe where she claimed a table with her backpack and sat on one of the red metal chairs, kicking her feet onto the one opposite her. Walking had been her go-to mode of transportation, so much so that in Berlin her feet had started bleeding after she'd walked a circle from her hostel in the south, hitting the memorial parks in the west, the Reichstag Building to the north, three museums on Museum Isle, and the World War Two relics in the east. She'd walked alongside the East Gallery Wall before stumbling back to her hostel, only taking a break when it started raining and she had to admit she was lost.

Stretching her ankles, Julie pulled out her phone and sent a quick text to her dad with her whereabouts. She still hadn't spoken to her mom, not since their big fight in July over how they'd both handled the death of Julie's little sister Hannah. But Julie knew a young woman traveling the world for several months — alone — was risky, and while she had no desire to speak to her mom just yet, she didn't want her parents to worry too much. She sent a quick text to her best friend Ella, whose housewarming New Year's Eve party she'd missed. She sent a text to Rachel, her other best friend who ran Maven Media, the company Julie used to work at with Ella. Then she sent a text to Ben, her third best friend, and the one who had helped her work through her emotions about her sister.

And her feelings for Anthony Russo.

She felt her body clench at the thought of his blue eyes and black hair. The way he always made her laugh. The slope of his broad shoulders trailing down to muscled arms that knew how to hold her. The way she'd left him after the most intimate night they'd had together, when she felt in her bones they were meant to be together.

But instead she said it had been a mistake.

Julie tried to fight the fear that the real mistake had been letting him go, instead trying to hold onto the idea that if they were meant to be together, they would be. That is, if she still wanted him after this month's long trip. And if he was able to forgive her.

After sending her texts, she opened Instagram. She had most of her travel pictures saved in drafts, so she posted one that made her life look perfect before scrolling through everyone else's perfect pictures. Julie was learning to be gentle with herself about what her life had looked like, what shape it was currently taking, and the way it would end up after everything was said and done. She was learning to be grateful, to not be so concerned with what everyone else thought. She'd done that after Hannah's death, and it had landed her at a school she wasn't thrilled with and with a job she didn't love.

But scrolling through her feed and landing on a group picture of that stupid holiday party was another level of self-work she wasn't ready for. Not when Anthony's arm was around Ruby Delacey, Maven Media's publicist for TV, Film, and Media. Not when Ruby's head was leaned against his chest. Julie couldn't help noticing Ruby's cleavage was better than her own, couldn't help knowing Ruby had a sweet gap tooth when she smiled. Couldn't help knowing her taste in music was better than Julie's, not when Ruby's desk sat next to hers at the office. At least it used to.

Stop.

Julie was doing everything she was working so hard to quit. Comparing looks, jobs, men.

She shut her phone, fixed her blonde ponytail, smoothed her shirt over her yoga pants. Pulled out a book in English she'd nabbed from one of the German hostels. Tried to read through the overwhelming feeling that her trip had been a mistake.

3

Anthony gazed at the rug beneath his feet, tracing the outline of the large sun and stars with his eyes while the rest of the band debated which song to start with. Their manager, his dad, had booked their first recording session at the famed Threshold Recording Studios. But after meeting with the sound engineers, they were debating switching the recording lineup from song order to doing the more upbeat songs first, before everyone got tired from recording.

He ambled over to the keyboard against one of the three windows looking into the sound booth. The keys called to him, anxious to be played. It was easier than the guitar. After his accident last year and the brain trauma he'd sustained, Anthony had to essentially relearn playing instruments. He'd tried the regular route of sight-reading but kept hitting a wall. His brain didn't work that way anymore, going blank at each note head and flag flourish. His neuropsychologist had told him to give himself permission to relearn in whatever way worked best.

Cue his auditory memory.

Once he'd let go of the expectation of the musician he used to be and started working on the musician he had to be, he'd been able to relearn Eternal Youths music by ear. While Gideon was the main songwriter and rhythm guitarist, Anthony was the lead guitarist. But his fingers weren't as fast on the guitar as they used to be, so this new album would rely more on his piano skills.

He didn't mind. There was something soothing about the piano. The band's first album, *Halo*, released last year and was more indie rock. This next album would have saxophone, thanks to their new band member Max Buchanan. Anthony and Gideon had founded the band back in college with the help of their friends Lucas Barre, the drummer, and Ryan Williams, the bassist. They were more like brothers than anything, especially given the shit he and Gideon had put the band through.

"Hey, Ant?" Max's deep voice came from behind

Anthony. He sighed before turning to face the saxophonist, stopping himself from doing a double take. Max had recently shaved his long dreads, the change still an adjustment. "Ant, we're gonna start with the new song *Summer*, feel it out and see how easy it is for us to get into a groove." Max turned, his slouchy jeans and loose knit cardigan out of place against the rest of the band.

Anthony sat at the keyboard. One of the recording rooms jutted into the room, creating an L-shape with the keyboard at the foot, the guitars and bass lining the stem, and the drums at the top. A Baldwin acoustic piano stood behind the keyboard, in view of the rest of the room and directly in front of the sound booth full of engineers and executives. Anthony's view was of the empty recording room, which hid the band. He preferred that. He could focus on the music, his fingers, without getting wrapped up in what everyone else was doing. And he wouldn't have to see the red electric strapped across Gideon, a color that was reminiscent of the curly haired woman from the New Year's party.

If Anthony thought giving Julie Milligan a second chance to break his heart, which she promptly did, was the biggest mistake of his life, he was dead wrong. Julie had left a hole in his heart, and sleeping with someone like Ruby Delacey should've eased his pain. But instead, Ruby had made the space Julie left behind more cavernous. He'd never be able to fill the hole, and trying to fill it with meaningless sex only made it worse. Like he was disrespecting what he and Julie had had.

Which was bullshit, since all they'd had was a casual fling years go and one perfect night that summer. Lucas started tapping out the tempo on the bass drum as Anthony pounded the piano keys, causing the count to stop.

"K, guys, we ready?" Ryan strummed the bass, throwing Anthony a look.

Anthony grumbled something resembling a yes before setting his fingers on the keys, trying to focus. It was the song they'd released as a single, the one where Anthony had created a simple piano loop when stuck at rehab before the band had left for the festival tour that summer. Lucas counted down, and Anthony played his part. Keeping it separate from what the others were doing. No matter how many times they'd practiced, Anthony still felt anxious and unsure when playing in front of people. Like he would forget his lines and everyone would laugh at him.

But he pulled through, keeping count in his head

with his eyes closed. He'd found looking at his fingers just confused him more and figured he should take his doc's advice of letting the old Anthony go.

It was rough, but they got through the song. Anthony stretched his arms before playing the song as quickly as he could without messing up. It was something his dad had suggested, once the appointments with the neuropsychologist stopped after his tests came back normal. They'd recommended music therapy that supposedly would do the double duty of helping him relearn music and work through the trauma of the accident and addiction.

Yeah, they could go fuck themselves.

Anthony was done with doctors. He was done with tests and wondering what was wrong with him. He was done relying on other people.

He was done opening himself up.

4

Goa was everything Julie had expected.

She was torn between loving the crash of the clear blue ocean waves and wanting to end her time there early thanks to the tourists and wild nightlife. Julie was glad her hotel was in South Goa where it was a bit quieter and only steps from Zumbrai Beach; the saltwater breeze came in through her open windows, giving her space to breathe.

The individual cottages of the hotel each boasted a balcony with her favorite scent, surrounded by lush teak and coconut trees. Each cottage was made up of one bedroom; Julie's own paneled room was small — cozy — and lit gold from the sun on the bronze wood. Her striped twin bed was nestled in a nook with two windows. A private bathroom sat off the main door, an armoire on the other side. It was bare.

It was perfect.

Julie stepped out on the balcony and stretched beneath the setting sun, the sky cast in an orange lavender. Closing her eyes, she felt the heat settle on her skin, a gentle warmth before the heaviness of humidity started to set in in the early spring. The wind running through the coconut and banyan trees sounded like a river, her hair moving with its flow. This had been a perfect stop after her colder travels in Europe. After her desperate attempts to make the life she'd built fit the person she wasn't sure she was. She hadn't been sure about the party scene she'd heard so much about and had only booked her stay here for a week. But now Julie was wondering if she should extend her stay before continuing onto Delhi and then onto the small mountain town her old co-worker Priya had told her about.

Stop.

Opening her eyes, Julie took in the rustling trees and ocean waves crashing. Part of her whole idea to take off and explore was to give herself space to grow. Each city had been given an intention, although the cities had ultimately given her new ones.

Amsterdam had taught her about her bad habits, more specifically her knack for spinning herself up.

And that's what she was doing.

Everything was already in place, she just needed to let go, which each city had been able to help with in their own way. But being in India, Julie wanted to release more than just the need to have a plan that went right. She wanted to find a sense of inner peace, where she didn't care so much about what everyone thought. Where she could find the life she actually wanted to live instead of the one she thought her parents had wanted for her.

Julie stretched along the balcony rail. She hadn't spoken to Ella in a few days, unable to bring herself to ask her best friend about the party and the stupid picture of stupid Anthony and stupid Ruby.

Not that she should care.

Julie thought about that morning after that perfect night, after a summer of learning Anthony's dreams and fears. When the pit in her stomach of everything feeling so right but so wrong had spurred her to say the words that would seal their fate.

It was a mistake.

She had no idea who she was or what she wanted. And she broke his heart. Hell, she'd torn it out, stomped on it, thrown it away.

She turned away from the bliss of South Goa. Padding across the wood floors to her bed, Julie pulled out her phone to double-check her itinerary. In two days she left for Delhi. There was no point worrying about things with Anthony.

She'd ruined things with the only man she'd ever been able to envision a life with.

Time to let go.

5

Anthony grabbed a Coca-Cola, enjoying the metallic tang as he listened to his dad in their living room, talking with the band about which upcoming tour to join: Arctic Monkeys or Imagine Dragons.

Feeling his phone vibrate, he pulled it out of his pocket. He couldn't think of anyone who would be texting him right now — everyone he loved was in the same room.

Except Julie.

Not that he still loved her. Not after what she did.

He shook his head trying to clear the image of her bright sapphire eyes, the gold glow of her skin, and opened the text notification from an unknown number.

Hey! It's Ruby, I had a great time the other night. :)

Fuck.

Anthony pocketed the device and grabbed his soda. A problem for another time. Ambling into the living room, he sat on the arm of the chair Ryan was occupying. He looked at the rest of the guys sitting on the couch, his dad standing in the wide doorway leading to the kitchen. Tried to pick up where in the conversation they were.

"Okay, but since we have Max we fit more with Arctic Monkeys." Lucas fixed his topknot, running his hands over the shaved sides of his head to gather the long pieces on top.

"Right, but Imagine Dragons is more mainstream." Ryan tapped his fingers on the chair. "I mean, wouldn't that be the best career move?"

"Not if we want to sell out." Gideon shook his head, brushing past Tom to grab something from the kitchen. Max stayed on the couch, stroking the scruff along his jaw.

"What do you think, Anthony?" Tom looked to his son. "We have to let them both know either way by end of next week."

Anthony could hear Gideon in the kitchen rummaging through one of the pantries, the loud banging evidence of Gideon's own thoughts on the matter. Anthony took a sip from his can. Their first album moved from a youthful indie rock into something a bit softer, ending with songs that capitalized on Max's soulful sax. The modern twist they'd given those last few songs paired well with some of the current pop songs on the various Top lists, and the new album was incorporating more of that. He took another sip to buy himself time.

He actually felt their music would be great paired with a female pop star — maybe Taylor Swift — but knew they needed a stepping stone. Arctic Monkeys was definitely indie rock. Imagine Dragons was pop rock.

"I take it neither isn't an option?" Anthony looked around the room.

"No. We have these two offers to work with."

Anthony sighed.

"But wouldn't Imagine Dragons be selling out? We're not pop," Gideon called from the kitchen island.

"But we're not strictly indie rock, and I'm wondering if branching out with a pop band will give us new listeners outside of our bubble. I think instead of going with Arctic Monkeys and playing to, say, 10,000 people we know will like our stuff and who have probably already heard of us, we should play to 10,000 new people with the hope that 5,000 of those new people will join the 10,000 from Arctic Monkeys that are already fans."

"I'm inclined to agree with Ant on this one," Max chimed in, his voice low but strong. "And I think that would give us more opportunities to team up with other artists that would better suit our sound, especially as it grows. We just have to make sure our sound doesn't go full-on pop — that's not us."

The guys looked around the room as Anthony felt his phone vibrate again. He listened to them debate the merits of each tour as he pulled out his phone, seeing that same number.

Ruby.

He clicked through to the text.

What are you doing tonight? :)

6

Coming out of the Delhi airport, Julie was greeted with a smog that fell against her skin like a blanket. The thick air settled in her lungs as it cast a yellow glow to the plaza, the constant array of car and scooter horns a backdrop to this surreal place. People milled about. Some men kept asking her about car service. Others just stared as she walked past, shifting her backpack high on her shoulders. Her old coworker, Priya Somari, was from Mumbai and had given her all sorts of tips for navigating the hectic Delhi airport, including where to find the flat rate taxi to the next terminal for her flight to Dehradun.

She politely but sternly told the taxi drivers no as she made her way to the kiosk. After paying and getting her ticket for her driver, Julie climbed into the designated car. She clutched her bag, looking around the bare metal interior. The night cast deep shadows in the back, the clank of the old engine startling her. The driver made no pauses getting out of the terminal, almost hitting several other cars while laying on his horn.

Wow.

Getting in and out of Goa seemed far away, and much calmer. But it seemed everyone here — west or east coast — drove with quick starts and stops, weaving and ducking between lanes.

And horns.

Lots and lots of horns.

The ride seemed to take forever, considering she was supposed to just go to another terminal of the Delhi airport. Julie looked out her window. They were on a highway, billboards and city lights passing by. Panic gripped her. Now she was completely unsure she was actually headed in the right direction. She clutched her backpack closer, running through what was happening, what could happen, and how she could escape.

And then the sign for Terminal 1 passed by. Julie relaxed as they wound their way to the right terminal. It was something she'd never get over while traveling alone. Some places — like Dublin — seemed easier than others. Others, like Paris, seemed more difficult. She had a man follow her back to her hostel. She had another man come up, put his arm around her shoulders, and try to kiss her. Here, she was trapped in a car with someone she didn't know.

Entering the new terminal, she was faced with fluorescent lighting, white tile, and few eating options. There was still a couple of hours until her flight to Dehradun, where she'd had her hotel set up a car to take her the hour-long drive to the small holy city of Rishikesh. Priya had told her it was a hidden gem of a Himalayan mountain town, split in half by the Ganges River, and held many Instagrammable spots. Julie was more in it for being by the river and surrounded by ashrams, and hoped she wasn't holding high expectations for the town.

Time passed without her knowing until it came time to board her next flight. The passengers were shuttled across the tarmac, where they boarded the charter flight. Julie had laughed to herself at the fifteen-minute drink service mid-air, a seemingly pointless amenity given the forty-five minute flight. When she finally managed to get off the plane from her middle seat, she was stunned at the difference between Goa and Delhi. Mountains rose in the distance, curved to a dull peak. The sun was just beginning to peer over the mountain's hips, an orange so bright and clear, Julie's breath caught. A light mist collected around the waist of the peaks, outlined by the dusty sky.

Julie hauled her bag and caught up with the other passengers heading to the small airport. But she kept looking over her shoulder, the sun climbing its way up the back of the mountain, ready to view the world. It moved more quickly than Julie had ever seen the sun move, and she couldn't help but feel the magic in the air.

She was right where she belonged.

7

Anthony couldn't tamp down the anxiety that what he was doing was a mistake. Not because shutting Ruby down was the right thing to do, but because he probably shouldn't be meeting her in person.

If there was one thing his father had taught him, it was how to treat people — but women especially — with respect. And regardless if his relations were one night or a few months, Anthony always ended things with someone in person.

He sat in the coffee shop, spotting the bounce of red curls in the sunlight streaming through the front window. Ruby's smile was wide as her heeled boots clicked their way to him, shedding her coat. Anthony got an unwanted eyeful of her chest when she leaned down, giving him an even more unwanted kiss on the cheek before taking the seat across from him.

He'd thought it'd be unwanted, but the intimacy of a peck on the cheek touched a part of him that hadn't been reached in months.

"Thanks for meeting up." His voice cracked as he reached for his coffee. "Can I get you anything to drink?"

"Oh, sure. I'll have a vanilla bean latte with whipped cream and a chocolate drizzle." Ruby's face was glowing, her freckles filling the sky of her skin. She played with her hands on the tabletop as Anthony went and got her drink, trying to keep the sweet concoction straight when giving the order and trying not to spill the mountain of whipped cream when he set it in front of her.

He stared into the hazel eyes before him, a world apart from Julie's icy blue ones.

Arctic eyes he should never see again, given how she'd broken him.

Which meant maybe — just maybe — he should actually give someone like Ruby a chance. Julie had shown Anthony that he did, in fact, want a relationship. At least with the right person. He liked how easy it was to build a friendship with someone, how comforting it was to have that consistent person in his corner.

"So... How was your week?" he asked. Gotta start somewhere.

"It was pretty good, thanks." Ruby's smile grew even wider, the gap between her two front teeth the star of the show. "How was yours?"

"Not too bad, the band's back in the recording studio. Getting our second album ready."

"Oh, right! I forgot you were in Gideon's band. Man, him and Ella are inseparable."

Anthony cocked his head, wracking his brain for how she knew his family. "Yeah, they are. I'm sorry, how do you know them again?"

"Oh, I work with Ella. I manage Maven Media's TV and Film clients, but we're also working on adding other clients who work in other media outlets."

Anthony felt his heart drop into his stomach.

"You... You work at Maven Media?"

Ruby laughed. "Um, yeah? Why, is that too close to Ella?"

He just stared at her. She had no idea just how close he was to Ella. And he was mentally kicking himself for not finding out who Ruby was before sleeping with her.

Before trying to talk himself into being with someone other than Julie.

"Anthony?"

"Sorry, I — I forgot I have a band meeting. I have to go." He threw her a quick smile, moving out of the booth quicker than he'd ever moved before. He didn't look back as he rushed outside, the January cold hitting him like a ton of bricks. The wind tunneling between the New York skyscrapers was dramatic, whipping his hair and pushing his body back where he'd come from.

No. He would never go back.

Anthony knew he shouldn't care how hurt Julie would be by the fact he'd slept with her coworker.

But if Ruby thought she was too close to Ella for him, he knew the reality was she was too close to the only woman he'd ever loved.

8

The Ganga ran over Julie's feet, the marble steps of the ghat warmed by the high sun. She held her face in her hand, eyes closed to the vividness of Rishikesh. She'd never known color before this little town, with its faded salmon buildings and sadhus — holy men — clad in orange robes reminiscent of that first morning sun when she disembarked the plane in Dehradun. The Ganga changed from a glacial blue to a vibrant turquoise to a warm mint, the light streaking the waves with gold. At sunset, the water took a purple cast, lavender like the sky. The emerald trees lining the cobbled street gave shade to blue metal tea stalls, cows every color of brown, stray dogs ranging from white to tan to black.

Opening her eyes, Julie smiled and watched a

large family bend down to offer thanks to the holy river. The children screamed and giggled as the icy water touched their skin, women wrestling with those tiny waving limbs as the men made prayers to Ma Ganga. Mother.

She stood to leave, knowing she would have to confront her own mother at some point. To start to heal their relationship. Julie climbed the steps to the upper platform, slipping on her shoes and walking the narrow street back to her hotel. Her beloved sister Hannah came to mind. She would've been twenty-one now. She would've been in college, traveling, partying, figuring out who she was. Julie's hand went to her chest, trying to hold back the ache in her heart.

For ten years, Julie had pretended the loss of her sister had never happened. She'd avoided every topic of family, hid every picture. She'd taken care of her parents until they managed to get back on their feet, but by that time Julie had resolved to do whatever it took to make them proud. A good school, a good job, a good friend group, a good man. A good life. Until the ten year anniversary had rolled around that summer and Julie realized she wasn't actually happy with her life.

Except for Anthony.

He was the only piece that made sense. Her mom always badgered her about the lack of a boyfriend — Julie dated plenty of men, but her mom wanted just one. One that she approved of, one that would provide Julie with a good life. One that was funny, smart, successful, handsome. But Julie had always pushed back on that ideal. She wasn't ready for that; she needed freedom from the classes she hated, a job she didn't like, pressure she didn't want. So she'd never had a boyfriend. It was the one thing in her life that her mom could latch onto, and she did.

Julie climbed the steps of the small hotel, smiling at the young male staffers standing in the lobby. Some of them smiled back, some of them turned shyly away. Most spoke little to no English, but a couple spoke enough to answer questions or keep up small conversation. As much as she liked to be alone, there was something about making transient friends in each new place that filled the empty space she was still learning to love. Being more or less alone with yourself for months at a time, navigating winding streets and foreign public transportation, extricating yourself from questionable scenarios... There was nothing to be done but love yourself.

She shed her wool jacket and kicked off her shoes upon entering her room on the third floor.

The January air was chilly, only mitigated by the sun during the day. Nighttime was still frigid, requiring wool socks and many layers in the sparse bedroom. Julie pulled out her phone and climbed under the covers.

Ella, Rachel, Ben, her dad.

No Anthony.

Not that she'd ever expect to hear from him again.

She chewed her lower lip. He didn't want to hear from her, and she could never speak to him unless she ready to commit. If he'd ever give her another chance.

Julie sighed, calling Ella first.

"Hey, Jules! How's Rishikesh?"

Julie could hear the smile in her voice, her best friend shushing and laughing at a muted male voice in the back. Gideon. The soft click of a door shutting. Silence.

"Hey, El. It's amazing. A bit chilly, but I feel so... so alive. How are you?"

"Oh, I'm so glad." Ella hesitated. "I'm fine, things here are fine. Really loving having so much time with Gideon, just the two of us. I mean, he's with the band a lot since they're working on the second album. And I'm at Maven Media trying to find a new music publicist to take over on-site publicity so I can focus on stuff here in New York and tour with Eternal Youths this summer."

"That's awesome, I'm so happy for you. And again, I'm so sorry I wasn't there for your New Year's-slash-housewarming party. It looked like it was fun." Julie picked at the thin comforter.

"I'm more sorry I wasn't with you! I'd rather be traveling the world. Trust me, you didn't miss much. It was a sober New Year's party with people I spend almost all of my time with. We had to have our friends bring friends to fill it out." Ella pushed a laugh.

"What's up, El? It sounds like something's a bit off." Julie waited through the silence on the other end.

Ella sighed. "Well, I found something interesting out. And I was debating whether or not to tell you."

Julie's heart clenched. Knowing, fearing, what Ella was about say.

"In any case, I guess I've never been very good at keeping things from you." Ella took a deep breath. "I was talking to Ruby the other day, asking if she'd had fun at the party. I kind of noticed her and — and Anthony getting cozy towards the end."

No no no no no no no no no.

"I mean, you know, not too cozy. But... close. And, um, well... I guess they had a thing."

Julie felt the walls closing in, her lungs tightening.

"And then he'd asked her to coffee and ran out, saying he'd forgotten a band meeting. But, obviously, I know when the meetings are because of Gideon and they didn't have one when Anthony said they did. So, I don't know. But I thought maybe you should know they... you know."

Julie let her worst fear hang between them. Anthony moving on — as he should — but with someone Julie knew. With someone Julie liked.

"Wh—what did you say to her?"

"I was honestly so shocked, I think I just stared at her for a bit until she laughed. 'Cause she laughs at everything. But in any case, I asked her if she knew you two had a history. Lemme tell you, if I thought she was pale before I'd asked that, I was wrong." Ella snorted. "She had no idea about you guys. I asked her what she was going to do and she said she needed to think about it."

Julie hugged her knees to her chest, trying to process what she'd heard. She had no right to feel possessive, hurt, over him. She had no right to wish

Ruby would pick someone, anyone, but Anthony Russo. He was supposed to be hers.

He'd always been hers.

Except she'd pushed him away to find herself. Julie released the breath she'd been holding, thankful she was in a place like India to get her feet back under her after news like this.

Holding onto who she'd been didn't do any good for anyone. Holding onto what she had with Anthony six months ago was even worse. She needed to let him go. She was on this journey to grow, to learn. To move forward.

"Thanks for telling me. I'm going to have to sit on that one for a bit." Her voice sounded small to her. It reminded her of the times she'd finally broken down her walls to let people in. Except this time, there were no walls.

There was just her and her self-broken heart.

9

Anthony sat on the couch in his living room, guitar resting on his lap, Gideon pacing the living room. He strummed the strings, mentally running through the lyrics he'd just given Gideon. Gideon stopped with his hands on his hips.

"Okay, I like the line 'I got used to your shape beneath the sheets', but what if we changed it to 'I traced your shapes in the weak morning light'?"

Anthony looked at his cousin, the main lyricist for Eternal Youths. "Yeah, that works." He set the guitar on the couch beside him. Words had never been his thing, but after the shit Julie pulled, Gideon had encouraged he try writing about things. Emotions. Anthony ran his hand through his hair on the way to the kitchen, still speechless at how he'd broken down his walls to let her in, only to receive third-degree burns.

"Ant, what's up?"

He popped the cap on his ginger beer and took a swig. To tell or not to tell, that was the question.

Gideon watched Anthony while he grabbed a can of Coke and took a sip. Anthony could always read Gideon; he was relaxed but a little worried, and the Coke was giving him something to do with his hands. As was the ginger beer for Anthony. He sighed, knowing Gideon would find out sooner or later.

If he don't already know, no thanks to Ella.

"I slept with Ruby."

"Ruby? Maven Media's Ruby?"

"Yep."

"Like, Ruby from the holiday party? Ruby that worked with Julie?"

"Jesus Christ, Gid, yes. That Ruby. Red hair, freckles, gap tooth. Laughs at everything, even when it's not funny and especially when she's nervous. Not the sharpest tool in the shed, but kind."

Gideon stared at him. "You seem to remember a lot about her for having seen her just that one night."

Anthony stared back, unsure what to say.

"For God's sake, dude. It was just one night, right?" Gideon asked.

"Yeah. Yeah… We just slept together one night. We met for coffee so I could end things."

"Why do I feel like there's a 'but' in there?" Gideon's dark blue eyes narrowed. "Anthony, talk to me. What's going on?"

"I — I don't know." Anthony sighed, taking his bottle with him to the couch. He took a swig, the sharp ginger a nice distraction from the ice cold of the bottle, so reminiscent of his life before the accident.

"It was weird. Being with someone other than Julie." He stared at the coffee table, littered with music magazines and stacks of books his dad always meant to start. "And I know that sounds crazy. I have't been with anyone since she ended things. And for a minute, I didn't think I'd ever be able to. But Ruby was funny, and sweet. And when we met for coffee, she kissed me on the cheek. And it was so… nice. That intimacy." He chewed his lower lip, avoiding Gideon's gaze.

"But…"

"But… I miss Julie, man. And I know I shouldn't, and I don't know why I do. I mean, I hate her sometimes. I really fucking hate her. And then I'll see something that reminds me of her, and I just miss her."

Gideon moved the guitar and sat beside him. Anthony clenched his jaw, feeling the sting behind his eyes, still refusing to look at his cousin. He couldn't remember the last time he'd cried in front of someone. He didn't need to start now.

"Have you spoken with Julie?"

"Not since that day."

Out of his periphery, Anthony saw Gideon nod his head. "What do you want from me — advice on Julie, or advice on Ruby?"

Anthony scratched his thigh, feeling the scrape of skin beneath denim. A knife against a plate.

"Both." He looked at Gideon. "Please."

10

The hotel was quiet for mid-morning as Julie padded down to the small restaurant on the ground floor. She smiled at two of the servers sitting at the table where they housed water pitchers, menus, a credit card machine. The four dining tables were spread out as much as possible. One wall sporting a TV that was almost always turned off, the opposite wall half made of glass that looked out on the front desk.

Julie took a seat at one of the back tables, facing out towards the glass wall and door that showed the dusty side street. There was a large concrete wall, crumbling, separating the street filled with cows and stray pups from a manicured ashram garden. Occasionally monkeys scurried along the top, careful to avoid pieces of glass left there to deter them. Julie smiled, loving how every shop keeper, every passing scooter, worked in tandem to keep their strange ecosystem running.

The men working there knew she always started with milk tea, and she placed her breakfast order of banana porridge and peanut butter toast when they brought out her first cup. A sense of peace settled around her shoulders.

"Another beautiful day." The soft voice came from a white-haired head nodding to the sunny outdoors. The man sat, shoulders sloping over a belly encased in a white shirt, just showing under his open jacket.

"Hmmm, there seems to be an endless number of them."

His head threw back as he released a laugh. Julie smiled, already loving how full this stranger was.

"Well, I can't seem to disagree with you there. When did you get in?" He folded his hands over his loose pants, clear eyes piercing hers.

"A few days ago, but I'll be here for a couple weeks. How about you?"

"Oh, a few days ago. I come every year around this time, it's one of my favorite places in the whole world." The corners of his mouth lifted.

"It's becoming one of mine, too. Have you been many places?" Julie sipped her tea, wondering about this doughy man who seemed at once ages younger and ages wiser than what his late-60's suggested.

"Oh boy, have I." He laughed again, thanking one of the servers for his coffee. "I served in the military my whole life. But this is one of the few places I can call home. I support a boy at one of the orphanages, it's absolutely fabulous. Here, let me show you pictures."

Julie smiled as he pulled out his phone, showing her pictures of a young boy with a smile full of missing teeth. This man she so desperately wished was her own grandfather explained how the orphanage provided relief for single moms and women from abusive situations, how the founder was a good friend of his and placed an emphasis on education, complete with their own school for kids that didn't live at the orphanage. By the time he was done, Julie was halfway through her breakfast and he was beaming ear to ear over his finished plate.

"You can eat lunch there, they serve food. It's called Ramana's Garden. Just cross Laxman Jhula and go left, you'll see it. The profits go back into the orphanage. It was nice seeing you, I'm sure we'll meet again."

The man pocketed his phone, rising and moving behind Julie to the card machine. Julie finished her tea and looked out the window, mulling over his words and pictures. One of the beautiful things about traveling by herself was not having any plans or expectations. She could do whatever, whenever. Including taking the long walk to the northwestern quadrant of Rishikesh, the area most noted for shopping and yoga schools filled with westerners wanting the true yoga teaching experience.

Julie asked for another milk tea while checking the weather. Today would be dreary, cold, but in a few days the promise of spring was held. Perfect for a garden lunch.

11

The galaxied carpet in the recording studio was becoming a familiar work of art. Anthony took a break from counting the stars, stretching his neck while looking at the sky blue ceiling interspersed with soundproof panelling. The band and the sound engineers had spent an hour discussing which songs to start recording, and tensions had risen to the point of everyone taking a short break.

After the band had ultimately decided to go with Imagine Dragons for their next tour, Ryan and Lucas felt some of the songs needed to be reworked to appeal to a pop audience. Gideon, Anthony, and Max felt they should stay true to their work, and the followers of Imagine Dragons would either like them or they wouldn't. Tom had tried to push them to get things sorted before their next recording session.

But they hadn't. So now the producers could see the band struggle to get on the same page.

Anthony ambled over to the grand piano while the guys filtered out of the room. He practiced his scales, thankful to feel his fingers moving a little bit faster than they did last month. He knew he'd never be the musician he once was, but after recovering from addiction and a traumatic car crash over the past year, any progress was good progress.

The artificial ivory was cool beneath his fingers and didn't have that oily feeling keys usually had. They didn't remind him of being in rehab, trying to help his band with a new song while he couldn't even think straight. Trailing his fingers along the board, Anthony tapped a few chords before settling into a soft rhythm. He closed his eyes to the melancholy sound, feeling it reverberate through his fingers.

Julie.

Everything reminded him of her. Everything reminded him to let her go.

Anthony settled in a lower register, letting the ballad flow through him. The love he thought they'd built had been a glass house. She'd walked away, and he owed it to himself to let her. Every promise they'd made ended with their hearts broken, a shattered house. This would be his last offering, and then he'd be done with her. He'd move on, try to mend the pain in his chest. Try to rebuild the walls he'd so carelessly torn down to let her in. He let the notes drift to a close as he opened his eyes, shoulders sagging from a blanket of defeat.

"Ant?"

Gideon's voice was soft. Anthony turned on the piano bench to look at his cousin. The other band members stood around him, staring. He ran his fingers through his hair, trying to ignore the ridge of his scar while he thought of what to say.

"I was just playing. Are we ready to start?"

"That was beautiful, do you have lyrics?" Gideon crossed his arms.

Anthony shook his head. Lyrics weren't his forte, no matter how much Gideon — the band's true lyricist — tried to help.

"Alright, well if you could come up with some, I can go over them with you." Gideon walked over to the guitars, Ryan to the bass, and Lucas to the drums, while Max adjusted the sax hanging around his neck. Anthony made his way to the keyboard, but not before catching a small nod from his dad in the sound engineer booth.

"Alright, Ryan and I talked it over," Lucas started. "We'll stick to the original songs, no changes, and hope the majority of Imagine Dragons' audience likes it."

Ryan nodded. "I think we should rerecord *Summer*, since it was the single we released for the summer festival tour."

The song had been the one Anthony had tapped out on oily keys in the middle of his cold white room in rehab. It was the song his family had used to help him remember how much he loved music, even if his brain and his fingers fought back. Rerecording the song would help get everyone in the same headspace, and maybe he could find a way to spruce it up a bit more.

Anthony settled at the keys, shoulders hunched as he waited for the countdown. The ballad, the girl, still haunted his thoughts, but he had to believe that focusing on something more fun and upbeat would come as a necessary distraction.

He could hope.

12

The road back to the hotel was cobbled, winding its way through small homes, walled-off schoolyards, and cow pastures. Julie let the sound of the Ganga River fill her senses alongside the golden sun on her skin.

The sense of peace she'd felt every day since arriving hadn't dwindled. And the lunch she'd had at Ramana's Garden had now given her a sense of purpose.

Julie had followed the advice given by the white-haired man — Francis, she called him, after him being a follower of Francis of Assisi — and had visited the cafe run by the adjoining orphanage and school. She'd been greeted by a posted flyer asking for volunteers, and she'd taken those words with her while she sat with her food. The end of her meal became her asking the various workers how she, too, could volunteer.

Now she was on a mission to return to her hotel and fill out the online application.

She saw the familiar sights of her neck of the woods, reaching the hotel sooner than she'd expected. Smiling hello at the front desk workers, Julie bounded up the steps to her room, taking off her shoes and immediately throwing open her iPad. She skimmed the volunteer information document; she could stay at her current hotel and go to the orphanage every day to help, for a month minimum.

Chewing her lower lip, Julie thought of the responsibilities. Six or seven days a week, 7:00 a.m. to 4:00 p.m. Kids.

The last child she'd really worked with was her sister, Hannah. And that was almost eleven years ago.

But Julie missed the insight kids had. The unique space of growing, changing, they occupied. Before she died, Hannah had always asked questions. Sometimes they were simple. Sometimes they touched on things Julie had either never thought of or wouldn't have the answers to until she was older.

And now Julie was older, and she wished she'd

had more time with Hannah. More time to explore those questions. More time to laugh and argue and love.

Right now, she could do whatever she wanted, when she wanted. A freedom she'd fought for when she gave up her job as a lawyer at her best friends' company. A freedom she'd had the immense pleasure of exploring for the past four months.

A freedom she wanted to part with in order to help those sweet faces she'd caught glimpses of during her sun-filled lunch, the peals of laughter floating around her.

Julie opened the volunteer application, filling in the blanks with the same intensity — the same gung-ho attitude — she'd given her studies when becoming a lawyer.

Her fingers froze over the keyboard.

Next of Kin.

She hadn't spoken to her mom since their fight back in July. The fight where Julie's mom finally admitted she placed some of Hannah's death on Julie's shoulders. Julie could practically hear her mother's voice, dripping with condescension, if she were to tell her she was in India and volunteering at an orphanage.

Oh, that's rich. What, you think because Hannah's dead you can fix it?

Rich. Her mother loved that word, used it with a fake laugh to make her point. No, she couldn't use her mom.

Julie thought of her dad. He used to be larger than life, and not just with his height. But he'd become withdrawn, resigned, over the years. He almost always looked at her with pity. Like he knew the uphill battle of Julie's mom was a lost cause. She sighed. If she used him, and the orphanage reached out, he couldn't not tell her mom.

She'd come back to that section.

The rest of the application went slower, medical details and work experience. Degrees and short answer questions. The reference section gave her pause. Julie needed two people who could vouch for her. It had to be Ella and Rachel. Her two best friends, her coworkers, her second family. Putting down their info, she figured she'd call them at another time to let them know.

Scrolling back to the Next of Kin section, Julie sighed. She'd have to talk to her parents at some point. She just didn't want that point to be now. Pursing her lips, tapping idly at the keyboard, she mentally scrolled through the people in her life.

Priya, Ruby, Anthony, Gideon, Ben.

Coworker, coworker, ex who slept with second coworker, bandmate of ex and fiancee of best friend, almost brother.

Duh.

She couldn't believe she hadn't thought of using Ben. They'd become friends back in college, thanks to Ella being their mutual connection, and he'd become one of her roommates back in New York City. He was the one who'd gotten her to open up about the loss of Hannah, about her insecurities of not knowing who she was. He never judged and always had sound advice. He was the brother she'd never had, but the one she'd always wanted. The one she'd always needed.

Julie put down his information and submitted the application.

13

Anthony opened the door, Ruby's shock of red hair tied up in a colorful scarf. She turned at the sound, throwing him a gap-toothed smile.

"Hey, you." Her hands fiddled in front of her, leather jacket rustling with the movement as she shifted her weight between both feet.

"Hey, come on in." Anthony stepped aside, catching a whiff of jasmine and lemon as she breezed past him. Her heeled ankle boots clicked on the hardwood floor, circling the room.

He swallowed, running his hand through his hair. Tracing the scar while he worked up the courage. He'd asked her here on the advice from Gideon. They needed to talk about... everything.

"Can — can I get you anything to drink?"

"Water, please."

Anthony walked over to the kitchen, grabbing two glasses of tap water while he watched her settle on the couch. He'd never had a girl over in this apartment before. He'd always thought it would be Julie, and only Julie.

This was not Julie.

He took a deep breath and passed off her drink. Watched her throat ripple as she took a sip, a stray curl of fire falling forward as she set the glass on the coffee table.

This was definitely not Julie.

He took a seat in the chair opposite her.

"Thanks for coming, Ruby."

She crunched her nose, changing the constellations of her freckles.

"Sure thing, Anthony. I think I know why."

"Why what?"

"Why you asked me here. It's because of — of Julie, right?"

Anthony felt the wind get knocked out of him at the sound of Julie's name leaving her lips. He sighed, knowing the only way through this was complete transparency.

"In short, yeah. I didn't realize you worked with her when we slept together. I really enjoy your company, but I loved Julie and she broke my heart. I don't know if we can see each other with that... there."

"I understand. I didn't know you guys dated. She was a bit secretive at work." She took a deep breath. "Look. I like you a lot, and we get along really well. I'm not looking for anything specific, but I would be interested in still seeing you. Julie and I... we were never really close, and she's been gone since September. I think, if you're up for something casual and seeing where it goes, it doesn't have to be a big deal. Julie doesn't have to make this a big deal. But, Anthony, that's up to you."

"Isn't there some sort of girl code?" Gideon had pushed Anthony to date around and move on from Julie, but the possibility of seeing Ruby hadn't really come up. Anthony had thought that was off the table.

"Yes, when girls are friends. We weren't really friends before and I literally haven't spoken to Julie since September. I like you, and I don't owe her anything."

Anthony watched her eyes, hazel in the early afternoon light streaming through the windows. He appreciated her honesty, her straight forward nature. He contemplated what it would look like, dating

Ruby. She was strong, a little ditzy, funny. She laughed at everything. It was easy being around her. Friends, with some sexual tension.

"I would be interested in getting to know you more. But I'd like to go slow. I know we already slept together, but I want to start over. I don't really know what I want."

She nodded. "That's fine. I'm not looking for anything super serious." She stood, grabbing her patterned shoulder bag. "I'm free Saturday. We can meet no sooner than 6 p.m., you pick the place."

Her footsteps were sure as she let herself out, throwing him a smile over her shoulder before closing the door behind her.

Anthony stared at the space she'd been in, anxiety creeping under his skin. He did want to see her, slowly. They didn't owe anything to Julie. He didn't even know when — or if — Julie would come back. And he certainly wasn't going to be caught waiting for her.

He knew that once he told Gideon, and Gideon told Ella, that's when he'd have to face this decision.

But in the meantime, he needed to figure out what to do for the first date he now had on Saturday.

14

Julie trailed behind Katherine, a volunteer-turned-administrator originally from Louisiana. Kat had been there for three years. That morning, they'd helped a few other volunteers get the seventy live-in students ready for school, where they would be joined by over a hundred other kids deemed at risk from the surrounding area.

"So, as you know, normally there's a bit of a waiting period for volunteering, but since it's not quite our busy season, we're a bit short staffed. We have you come here early the first week and stay until the end so you can get a feel for the schedule and tasks at hand. Since we got the kids ready for school, there's some time before they come home. Generally we have a scheduled rotation of duties.

One week you may be on morning duty, another week you could be on tutoring or homework duty. When it gets really busy, we may schedule you for cafe duty during the day."

Kat's long legs had brought them from the kids' dormitory to said cafe, situated beside the school. The cafe was set down a few steps, mahogany double doors with framed glass. The inside was huge, with stone and brick walls and at least six long tables to seat patrons, plus a large deck — also with multiple tables — overlooking the Ganga. It didn't open until 11 a.m., but Julie just wanted to get started.

They walked through opening the cafe, sanitizing, getting the oven preheated for the cooks who would be in charge of the more elaborate dishes. Kat went over the desserts that would be delivered and the simple foods volunteers prepared: muesli, shakes, salads. By the time they'd finished, the two scheduled volunteers and cooks had arrived. Kat led Julie outside to the field backing the orphanage complex. It took Julie a minute to realize the field was delineated.

"Do you grow your own vegetables?" She jogged to catch up to Kat, looking at her counterpart with excitement.

Kat laughed. "Yep, all organic. During the winter

months, we purchase produce from local vendors or have them delivered. But it's a great education for the students, and the volunteers tend to enjoy teaching the kids about the plants and food. Since winter is ending, we tilled the soil and the kids will be planting the seeds in the upcoming weeks. Follow me."

Julie was led through the rows, some fenced, all bare, to a small shed that had seen better days. It held netting, trowels, shovels, hoes, rakes, and all kinds of seeds. Kat gave a brief spiel, adding that the garden was usually left to more seasoned volunteers, before leading back to the school.

They entered a side door, a large room filled with tables. One side of the room held tiny chairs for the elementary school students, one adult chair per table. The other side had adult chairs for the middle school students.

"Due to the laws here, we can only provide education through 8th grade. After that, kids have to apply and be sponsored for their education through 12th grade." Kat crossed her arms. Her voice echoed in the cavernous room, her words laced with a hint of defeat.

Julie looked around, imagining these tables filled with kids of all ages, facing unimaginable home situations and needing to get their homework done.

"How — how often do the kids move up to ninth grade?" Julie's voice felt small, buried beneath the weight of the question. She was scared of the answer, and the look on Kat's round face when she turned towards Julie confirmed her fears.

"Julie, you will be faced with children who are lucky to eat once each day. And that meal is the one they get here, at school. You will be faced with children who are trying to avoid being used for prostitution, who have seen their fathers beat them and their mothers. You will be faced with boundless love, and a joy only children can harness. This is a hard place, but it's a loving one too. We get our kids through eighth grade, and then it's completely up to sponsorships. We're currently able to sponsor twenty students in high school and three in university. Every year, that number grows. And that has to be enough."

Kat started towards a door in the back, her attention switching to the school subjects and what teaching materials were held behind the door. Julie followed, thinking over what Kat said. She wondered what Kat had lost to bring her here, and what she'd found that kept her here.

15

Anthony tried to ignore Gideon's face, instead taking a last look in the mirror and smoothing out his hair.

"Ant, I think this is a really bad idea."

The reference to the impending date with Ruby wasn't needed. Anthony could see the disproval all over his cousin, from the set of his mouth to the way he leaned forward on the couch, elbows resting on his knees.

"I know, but I need to see where this goes."

"Are you sure you're not bored? Are you sure you're not so desperate to be close to Julie that you'll fuck one of her friends?"

"Fuck you, man." Anthony whipped around, grabbing his jacket. "You don't know jack shit."

"Oh, I don't know jack shit?" Gideon laughed, a

cold wind in the small apartment. "I know Julie broke you. I know you came to me for advice on what to do once you found out Ruby works at Ella's company. I know that no matter what you tell yourself, you miss Julie. You want her, you might even convince yourself you need her. I told you to end things with Ruby — we both know this isn't going to end well. But you know what? It's your own fault. So when it goes to shit, you're on your own. I tried to help." Gideon stormed down the hall, slamming the door to the bathroom.

Anthony slammed the front door, making his way out of the building and to the jazz club he'd found in the West Village, off Ruby's subway line. The walk from the East Village was long, the air brisk. A perfect time to clear his head.

Dodging the people heading to their own Saturday night plans, Anthony tried to temper the fire raging inside him. Fuck Gideon. He'd told Anthony to move on from Julie, to date and take his time healing. He didn't know Ruby and Julie weren't really friends. He'd clearly forgotten Julie had been gone for five months. An apparition. A dream.

Anthony's heart swelled with the pain, the memory, of Julie. It helped thinking she almost didn't exist anymore, being halfway around the world with no real idea of when she'd be back. It helped knowing that she was so clouded, she'd brought Anthony down when he'd worked so hard to build himself back up. He needed to move on, and he needed something fun and casual. He already liked Ruby, so why not casually date her?

Before he knew it, he spotted the tall redhead outside of the jazz club. She'd straightened her hair, a dress hugging her slim body beneath a black coat. A scalloped edge highlighted the fair skin of her cleavage. As soon as she smiled at him, Anthony felt himself relax. At the very least, they were friends. And his friend looked gorgeous. He told her as much, giving her a tight hug and enjoying the warmth of her fragrance.

He placed a hand on the small of her back, feeling the rise of her ass against his pinkie as he gave the host their cover fee. Ruby's stilettos clicked on the granite floor as she led him towards the back of the narrow venue, picking a table beside the large piano. Anthony was surprised they were able to sit there. He specifically made their meeting time early enough to get seats at the small, hidden club, but he hadn't expected to be so close to the music.

"I've never heard of this place before." Ruby smiled at him, a blush creeping along her porcelain cheeks as she removed her coat and sat. The small candle made her skin glow as she flipped through the small menu, chewing the inside of her mouth while she contemplated what to order. Anthony wanted to touch her hair, a sunset waterfall. He wondered if it would slip through his fingers like water, burn his skin like fire.

Her laugh broke through his thoughts, and he smiled.

"What?"

"They have funny drink names." She passed him the menu, a manicured nail pointing at the cocktail list. "I'll have the Shaken But Not Forsaken, since there's a two-drink policy. And maybe the cheese platter? I'm feeling a bit hungry."

Anthony nodded, knowing he'd stick to seltzer for his drink order and picking a meat, olive, and nut platter to go with the cheese platter. Anthony gave the server their order.

Ruby rested her chin in her hand, staring at him.

"I'm really glad we were able to talk things through." Her voice was soft.

"Me, too."

"I don't know much, but from what Ella said, you and Julie were really serious and then... she kind of pulled the rug out from under you? You don't need to tell me anything you don't want, but I want you to know you can always talk to me as a friend."

Their drinks arrived, Ruby's wide smile causing the server to blush. Anthony sipped his seltzer, wishing — not for the first time and certainly not the last — that it was something stronger. Like a gin and tonic.

"I appreciate that, Ruby. Thank you. I'm glad we were able to come to an understanding and keep things casual."

"My mom always said the easiest way to mend a broken heart was by finding someone else." She sipped her Scotch cocktail, eyeing him over the rim of her glass. Her eyes were brown in the dim light, not the fragmented hazel that glowed in sunlight. Not the icy blue of Julie's.

"Your mom might be the wisest person around." Anthony took to his seltzer again, wondering what his mom would say in this situation. Not that she'd offer him anything. She still hadn't responded to that message he'd sent her back in July. Not a word.

"You okay?" Ruby tilted her head, hair cascading over her shoulder. Anthony watched as a musician sat at the piano, another standing behind his upright bass.

"They're about to start." Anthony threw her a

small smile before turning his attention to the duo before them, occasionally glancing at Ruby's bare shoulders, imagining her delicate skin beneath his calloused hands.

Wondering if they got close enough, who would break who.

16

Volunteering at an orphanage made time fly. That morning, Julie had to take a second glance at her calendar when she realized it was already early February, a little less than a month after starting her journey at Ramana's Garden.

Julie glanced at the empty homework room, waiting impatiently for the kids that would soon bombard the tables. She had her little group of second graders she worked with English homework for the first forty minutes, before moving onto an even smaller group of eighth grade girls for the last forty minutes of the allotted tutoring time.

Julie immediately felt complete as she watched the stampede of students in their red and blue uniforms and listened to the sound of yelling, laughter, squealing, Hindi mixed with English, all pushed through the doors. A few of the other volunteers took their stations at various subject tables split between the elementary students and the middle school students. There were fewer kids here than those that attended the actual school; most of the children from the local villages had to return home to help their family. But the seventy students who also lived at the home were required to come here, so every afternoon the sounds of a hundred kids and young adults filled the space.

Her ten charges, aged seven to nine, took their seats at the table, beaming up at her.

"Hi, Miss Julie." The chorus of their sweet voices warmed Julie's heart.

"Hi, my friends. How was school today?" She always started their tutoring with that; she wanted, needed, them to know someone cared. Julie laughed, trying to listen to ten excited kids at once while blocking out the surrounding din of students and tutors.

"Sounds like everyone had a nice day. What homework do we have?" Julie fixed her ponytail while the tiny hands searched their backpacks for the right papers. Some of the girls still stared at her blonde hair, but most had gotten used to the color.

Julie went over the collection of papers handed to her by Sanjay's grubby little hands. They were learning animals, and they all spent most of the time laughing while imitating the different noises.

"Okay, halftime!" Kat's voice rang through the room, followed by a couple claps. She smiled as the younger kids got their things together to head out, leaving the live-in kids with the volunteers. Julie hugged each of the kids she worked with, sad to see them go back to a life that was harder than anything she could imagine. When she'd first started, especially when she worked in the morning getting all these kids ready for school, she was horrified at the sheer poverty they carried on their shoulders and in their eyes. And these kids were luckier than most, taken care of by an orphanage they didn't live in. But these kids almost always had a smile, and Julie had to work through her own feelings of privilege to understand that there was only so much she could do. But she could always love, and that's what she did.

She stayed at her table as five girls took their seats, their English strong and their faces bright. Julie took a seat among them, always excited for this time with these young adults. They immediately pulled out their English and Northern India history papers. The rule had always been the sooner they finished their work, the sooner they could talk with Julie about things outside of school. Julie usually let them figure their work out themselves, unless she overheard something wrong or they asked a question. She always checked it over before claiming it done.

The girls moved quickly through their work, hardly addressing Julie. She watched them, ebony silk hair braided, fast Hindi interspersed with slower English. The occasional giggle. It never failed to amaze Julie how a teenage girl was a teenage girl everywhere, how she was so filled with love at their tenacity and insecurities and the sweetness still carried in their round cheeks, highlighted when they smiled.

Julie thought back to one of her days back at Maven Media. The awesome, very American company her best friends had founded. She'd been underlining and highlighting contracts for what felt like ages, and she had been annoyed. So she set down — no, threw — the highlighter at the stack of paper. The pen had bounced, bounced, bounced, rolled along the floor. The sound was hollow, loud, and Julie could do nothing but let it echo through her brain. Until Rachel had asked if she was okay.

So Julie did the thing most Americans did, and lied.

Peachy.

That was one of her favorite words. It still was, but now she could use it and mean it, all with a smile. She'd found something she loved.

"Miss Julie, we're done." Akhila passed over the papers. Her heart-shaped face was soft, her voice softer. Julie knew they shouldn't have favorites, and she really tried to stick to that, but there was something about Akhila that made it impossible. Julie got the sense she was much older than her twelve years. That she'd loved and lost and still managed to be kind. Gentle.

Julie took the papers, scanning the English homework. The girls were moderately proficient and only needed a couple of spelling corrections. The history papers were similar, but she couldn't do anything about the half that was in Hindi. Julie only knew enough to get by; no matter how hard she worked at more complicated sentences, she had trouble navigating the syntax. The girls sometimes helped, laughing as they did.

"Okay, we have fifteen minutes. What do you want to talk about?" Julie looked at each face. When she'd started, they'd all looked down at the table.

Now they all met her gaze, jumping over one another for a topic.

It landed on boys, as it almost always did.

Julie sighed, trying to turn their barrage of questions back on them.

She wanted to fall into their traditional, romantic way of dating. Of loving. She wanted to help these young women navigate love and heartache. She didn't want to talk about dating in America. She didn't want to talk about the casualties. She didn't want to talk about Anthony.

17

Anthony sat at the piano in the recording studio, playing through the ballad once more. Taking his time, letting each note reverberate through his body. It'd been a month of perfecting every song on their second album. They just had to do this last one and then it was done.

He and Gideon still hadn't really spoken since their fight in the apartment. Anthony had since gone out with Ruby several times, enjoying each time more than the last. He thought it was cute when she wrinkled her nose. He thought the fact she laughed at everything was sweet, even though it used to annoy him. He always tried to count her freckles, or make shapes in them, but he was never able to find the end. He liked how she smelled of jasmine and lemon, and tasted like honeysuckle and salt. They never spoke about serious things, but he was okay with that.

Julie had been the last person he'd done that with, and it hadn't ended well. He didn't need that with someone. Not right now.

The run-through of the ballad trailed off; it was as good as it was going to get. He'd given lyrics to Gideon, who'd worked on them privately. He gave his revisions back to Anthony, who then made minor tweaks that fit the sentiment better. But they never talked about it. He knew Gideon knew it was about — that it was a goodbye for — Julie. He knew when it released, Ruby would know it was also for the lost love of his life.

But he needed to do this.

He turned to Gideon, standing by the mic in the center of the galaxy carpet. Tom was hanging out in the sound booth, waiting to give the go ahead to record.

"Hey man, you ready?" Anthony's voice felt shaky as he addressed his cousin. He knew they'd have to clear the air at some point, but it always felt like Gideon was avoiding him. And Anthony hadn't felt like he had the bandwidth to deal with any fallout.

Sometimes silent tension was easier to manage.

"Yep." Gideon turned away from Anthony, hugging the mic between both hands. Anthony gave the thumbs up to his dad and the engineer through the window, waiting for the countdown.

He closed his eyes, playing the intro he heard in his sleep. He opened them at the sound of Gideon's baritone voice giving life to the lyrics, hearing the pain in Gideon's own voice at the detailed description of events, the way Anthony would never be able to erase Julie. The broken promises, the broken hearts. Anthony let Gideon's voice carry him through his own memories of golden skin, lush curves, and a wit that always threw him off. A cloud of vanilla rose that gave him warmth.

Anthony finished his part before Gideon, letting his voice haunt the silent room. Anthony turned to his cousin, hunched over the mic, eyes closed.

"I don't think we need to do it again, but we can so we have a few takes to work with." Tom's voice came over the speaker, the sound engineer's agreement faded in the background.

Gideon faced Anthony, his hand running through his hair. "Actually, what are your thoughts on background vocals during the last stanza? Either you and the guys, or maybe some soft female vocals?"

Anthony glanced at the men behind the glass. He could see their lips moving, but their faces gave nothing away. He cleared his throat and turned back to Gideon.

"I think it's worth trying."

"You did good on this, Ant."

The words took Anthony by surprise.

"Hey, guys?" Tom's voice came over the speaker. "We like the idea of background vocals. Let's record it once more just the two of you, and then we'll book a short session next week and get the rest of the guys in here, and some female vocalists. Sound good?"

The cousins agreed at the same time, giving each other a look of understanding before giving the engineer the go-ahead to count down. They may not agree on things. They may have things to work out. But they were family, and they were bandmates.

Anthony knew they had each other's backs no matter what, and that everything would be okay.

18

Lazy Sunday mornings were Julie's new favorite things. As much as she loved being at the orphanage, she loved the gentleness of no plans and no one needing her just as much. She laid in the firm bed in the sparse room in her quaint hotel, the door to the balcony open. A breeze blew through the screen door meant to keep out monkeys, the sound of scooter horns and joyous Hindi drifting with it.

She sipped the chai tea she'd ordered up, not wanting to brave the breakfast crowd that was slowly growing with each passing day. Francis had warned her February and March were peak times to visit the mountain town, and she noticed it most when she tried to eat in the little hotel restaurant.

It was nighttime in New York. Evening in

Chicago, where her mom and dad were probably getting ready for a silent dinner. Julie sighed, knowing she couldn't stay away forever. Knowing that, at some point, she'd have to figure out what was next, after her travels. Grabbing her phone, she knew Ella and Rachel would be able to help.

"Jules!" Ella's voice squealed on the other end. "Oh my god, I haven't heard from you in ages! How are you? Your pictures look amazing. Oh, Rachel and Ben are here, you're on speaker!"

Julie laughed. She'd usually been the excitable one in the friend group and Ella the slightly more introverted one, but since Ella had become engaged to Gideon it was almost as if they'd switched personalities.

"Hey, guys! Things here are good. The orphanage is amazing. These kids… I love them all so much and they've easily helped me as much as I've helped them. The weather is beautiful. Food is incredible. Um… Yeah. What's new with you guys?" She smiled into the phone, realizing how much she missed her friends. Her chosen family.

"We're so glad to hear it, Jules!" Ben's voice was in the distance. Julie could picture his floppy hair and brown doe eyes. "My job at the publishing house sucks but it's interesting. That's about it." He laughed his quiet, goofy laugh.

"Gideon and I are good, but I need you to come back to help with wedding stuff." Julie could hear Ella's happiness, and Julie's heart pained with just how much she missed home. "Maven Media is fine, we're keeping up with the clients. It's slowed a little, which has been nice." A slight pause gave Julie the familiar pit in her stomach, and she wondered if there was an update on the Ruby and Anthony situation.

But Rachel cut in before Julie could ask. "We miss you, Jules. Where are you headed next?"

"Nepal, Thailand, Malaysia." Julie bit her lower lip, not even sure she wanted to continue her journey. Those three countries meant at least two more months before she could go home.

"I mean, try not to sound so excited," Ella said, her voice carrying worry and only a hint of sarcasm. "Are you sure you're okay?"

"Yeah. Yeah." Julie took a deep breath. "I just... I just didn't realize how much I missed you guys. Like, I'm in my own little world over here and there's a whole life still happening over there."

"You know we'll always be here when you come

back," Ben said, always the reassuring one. "You'll always have a home, and we can find you a job."

"I know. Thanks, guys. I just don't know what that job would be."

It was silent on the other end until Ella spoke up. "I mean, you like the volunteer work, right? Because we've been wanting to start a nonprofit branch of Maven Media. We don't really know where to start, but when you come home we can talk about it." Ella was always the one with ideas.

"Oh El, yes!" Rachel's vibrancy translated through the phone. "That's a fantastic idea. And Jules, I promise we'll do everything in our power to make sure you never have to highlight another contract."

Julie smiled, this new idea clicking. Of course she'd have to find a job at a nonprofit when she returned to New York. Helping people was the only thing that felt good, right, that felt like she was born to do. Being able to do so at the company she loved, with the people she loved even more?

Yes, please.

"Is... is that even possible? Would we really be able to do that?" Julie wasn't sure what the financial standing of Maven Media was, or how many employees they now had. Her almost six months away had been blissfully detached from the goings on of the New York City rat race.

Except for Ruby and Anthony.

Julie's heart sank. She had built a life around being a lawyer, a job she told herself was her dream in order to make her parents happy. But her actual dream job was right in front of her. She just didn't know if she could do it, knowing Ruby would be there.

"Of course it is, Julie. As soon as you come home, we'll work it out," Rachel said.

Julie had been through so much: the death of her sister, the revival of her relationship with her parents. Good grades, good school, good job. She'd fought for everything she had. She'd given it all up and started over.

She knew she'd have to be strong again; she couldn't let Ruby stand between her and her dream.

She couldn't let herself place any blame on Ruby.

And Julie certainly couldn't let herself get in the way.

19

Anthony laid in bed, enjoying the feel of cool black sheets and late morning sunlight. He stretched out, taking up as much space as possible, feeling like things might be on the right track since his last night with Julie.

The band had been practicing backing vocals for the ballad, and everyone was getting more and more excited about it. Which didn't usually happen with ballads, let alone ballads from a pop rock band.

Ruby was still fine taking things slow. They'd mainly made out with a couple steamy moments, but no sex since New Year's Eve, and she'd relaxed into a calm manner around him, a welcome change to her almost franticly nervous energy she used to have. Getting to know her, spending time with her, was exactly what he needed.

He still needed to talk to Gideon about their fight, but things were almost back to normal. That was one thing about family — they would always be there.

Anthony sat up. If he got up too late, it felt like he'd lost his whole day. He was slowly approaching that line, the anxiety of missing time looming. Swinging his legs over the side of his bed, he stood and adjusted his briefs.

The only thing that could make this day better was coffee.

He checked his phone on the way to the kitchen. Since deleting almost every social media app from his phone back in September, there wasn't much to check. Tom was already out of the apartment doing who knew what, and he'd left Anthony a mug by the coffee pot. Anthony poured a cup, opening the New York Times Crossword app.

His phone dinged before he could start the day's puzzle, the name of the messenger almost causing him to spit out his precious first coffee sip.

Christina Scott.

His mom.

The notification slid back into the phone.

Anthony almost clicked the Facebook Messenger app to make sure her words were real, but he didn't want to seem too eager. He almost laughed at himself for that one. He'd been waiting to talk to his mom for over ten years. The message he'd sent back in July was simple, just asking if they could talk.

It took her over seven months to respond to her own son.

Anthony opened the app, forcing the inner insecure child he thought he'd parted with further down. Fuck her, if she thought he was too eager.

We should, honey. Thanks for reaching out. I live in Connecticut, where are you nowadays?

Okay. No mode of actual contact outside of the little messenger app. No phone number, email address, plans to meet. Just... Where do you live? And her stupid profile picture with her in the arms of a man, surrounded by two teenage girls.

Anthony pursed his lips, responding with New York City. Maybe he could catch her before she logged off so he wouldn't have to wait another half a year for another stupid question.

But at least she wanted to talk, which was more than he got when he was eighteen.

Too anxious to drink his coffee, Anthony stared

at the phone screen. An incoming message toned, and he raced to read it.

Ah, your father always loved New York. Would you like to meet in person or have a phone call?

Anthony didn't know what to make of her response. Wouldn't she want to see him? Wouldn't a phone call with her estranged son of ten years be... weird?

In person. Mom.

In case she needed a reminder of who she was talking to.

He waited for her response, but after ten minutes, it was clear she was gone.

Again.

His head buzzed with all the questions he had. Did she actually want to see him? Did she love her new family more than her old one? Did she want a relationship with him or was she trying to amend the fact that what she did was shitty?

Anthony tried his coffee once more, the cold bitterness almost choking him as he swallowed. He tossed it in the sink, not knowing how to move past the anxiety that now resided within him.

His day was fucking ruined.

Pacing the apartment, he had to push aside reaching out to Julie. Outside of his dad and Gideon, she was the only one who knew the details of his relationship with Christine. She was the only one who'd offered him a shoulder, an ear, some advice. But she was halfway around the world and didn't need to hear from her ex, no matter how close they'd been. Tom would be out doing band things all day, and he'd told Anthony he didn't want to know anything about where his ex-wife was. Anthony knew he could talk to Gideon, but he didn't know what he'd be interrupting now that Gideon lived with Ella and they were planning a wedding. There was too much to catch any of the other band members up on.

That left Ruby. Aside from also having to catch her up on his life, he didn't want to cross that personal line with a romantic partner. It was too soon.

Anthony stopped his pacing and looked around the empty apartment, realizing just how alone he was, wishing his life had worked out differently.

20

Julie hugged her students, her friends, lingering on Akhila before parting. She followed Kat into her office, shutting the door behind her with a soft click. Julie took a deep breath and faced her mentor.

Kat had taken a seat at her desk, shuffling papers around. Julie smiled to herself, surprised at how anxious she was to get back behind a desk.

"Sorry, give me one more minute," Kat said, distractedly going over a pile of papers. Julie looked around the bare office. There was a bookshelf on one side of the wall filled with nonfiction on raising kids, nonprofit business, and agriculture. There was one picture of a slightly younger Kat and a small boy, both of them smiling.

"Okay, what did you need?"

Julie turned to her boss. Kat wore a sad smile. She looked tired.

"Well, I wanted to talk to you about my time here. I think it's time for me to head home, but I'm not under any specific time constraints so I wanted to see what worked for you." Julie smiled and clasped her hands in front of her. She'd learned to temper her training as a lawyer, to come more softly to conversations when they were just conversations, not inquisitions.

Kat sighed and leaned back in her chair. "That's a shame, you leaving. But I understand. We're starting to get more and more applications since we're in the nice season, so really whenever you're ready to leave. I'd prefer if it was after another day or two so you can say goodbye to everyone. The group of girls you work with have really taken to you." She smiled. "Especially Akhila, the little sweetie. She'll be sad to see you go."

Julie felt her heart break at the thought of saying goodbye to her friend. "I would love to stay in contact with her, would that be possible? She could practice her written English if we were pen pals. I — I've learned so much by being here, about myself and about the world. I'm better, more full, for knowing her."

"Funny you say that. Her name actually means 'complete', and I think she'd say the same about you." Kat stood, pulling open her leatherbound planner. "So let me know when you have a date in mind, I like to do exit interviews. And truly, thank you so much for all that you've done." She held out her hand, and Julie grasped it.

Leaving the orphanage complex, Julie felt excited about her future for the first time... ever. She crossed Laxman Jhula, one of the bridges that crossed the Ganga, and started her forty minute walk back to the hotel. Knowing she could go home when she felt like it, knowing she could do work she believed in, was what her life was supposed to be about. Not the law degree she thought her parents wanted. Not the fancy job she thought she needed to be successful.

When she finally made it back to her hotel, she pet the puppies that hung around the front doors before bounding up to her room. Julie immediately called Ella. It went to voicemail and Julie realized it was still early morning in New York. She had to temper excitement until her friend called back, so she opened the calendar app on her phone to figure out when she could be home. She'd give herself two more days at the orphanage, three days to enjoy Rishikesh, and then she'd head home. The trip would take about twenty-four hours. Julie would be home by this time next week.

Relief settled inside her. She would still love to see Nepal, Thailand, Malaysia. But there were other things she felt called to do at this point in her life, and those travels would always be there. Knowing she'd be returning home with a purpose made this decision even more worth it.

She wasn't sure how the kids would take the news. Julie's heart broke. If there was one thing her volunteer experience had given her outside of a purpose for her career, it was the reinforcement that she wanted kids. Anthony had been the only man she'd ever been able to see herself marrying, the only one she could envision as a father. He was the first — and only — man that made her even consider having kids.

Her mind flitted to him and the awkward pause from Ella and Rachel on their previous phone call. Julie couldn't help but feel that he and Ruby were seeing each other. And she couldn't help but feel she had no right to be mad or upset, even when those feelings were supported by the one feeling she'd never been able to shed.

She'd let him go, and now it was too late to win him back.

21

The energy in the recording room was one Anthony hadn't expected for a ballad. The three women backing vocalists were joking around with Tom and Gideon. Ryan, Lucas, and Max were rehearsing their version of the vocals. They weren't intrinsically singers, so they'd really had to practice to get what they had. Anthony had sat out, knowing that he'd bring everyone down — thanks to the tone deafness brought on by his head trauma.

Sitting at the piano, looking around the room of everyone there to support him and each other, he almost regretted feeling like he wished his life had gone differently. He still hadn't told anyone about his mom reaching out, but she vowed to come to the city to see him.

Anthony scoffed. It was the least she could do.

But he was so thankful for the band, and everything they brought with it. The success and heartbreak and shame and love. He wished he didn't feel quite as lonely, but he lived a good life. After hitting rock bottom, it could only get better.

"Alright guys, let's get this wrapped," Nate, the band's record label rep, said before heading to the sound booth. He didn't usually come to the sessions, but Tom had shared a rough recording of the ballad and Nate wanted to hear the backing variations himself.

Anthony sat at the baby grand piano, keys cool beneath his fingers. Working through this song had helped him release things he'd been holding onto with Julie. He was ready to finish this last allowance, this last wallow. He was ready to feel like he was able to move forward.

The three women joined Tom and Nate in the sound booth, and the sound engineer Aaron counted down. Anthony and Gideon launched into their parts, Gideon still maintaining the necessary high level of emotion despite how many times they'd played this song. Lucas, Ryan, and Max surrounded a mic, waiting for their cue. Anthony heard someone come in early, and only one of them sounded decent once they got on the same page. When Gideon finished the main vocals, he and Anthony shared a look.

"So... yeah. We need to do that again," Tom said. "Ryan, you came in too early. And you and Lucas sounded a little... flat. Max, well done." Anthony watched his dad rub his face, leaving his hand over his mouth.

"Guys, we'll run through this twice more and then take a break before getting the ladies in here," Aaron said over the speaker.

The band settled back into their positions, Anthony starting on the intro once more. This time everyone came in at the right time, but someone sounded like a dying animal. Tom gave appropriate notes, and they tried a third time. The dying animal continued to live, the strangled notes giving Anthony a headache.

"I'm sorry, I can't." He pulled his hands from the keys, turning to face his bandmates. Lucas held his head in his hands while Max and Gideon laughed up a storm.

"I'm sorry, I'm a drummer. Not a singer." Lucas was trying to hide a smile, shaking his head. "I'll see myself out."

Tom came over the speaker. "Yeah, I think we should call it quits. Let's give it ten, and then please, please stay out of that room until after we record Sophia, Cora, and Reese."

The guys filed out of the room into the sound booth. Aaron played both takes, causing everyone to cry from laughter. Anthony and Gideon grabbed some water, still laughing as they reentered the music room with the next round of vocalists. The women huddled around the mic and immediately calmed themselves. Anthony and Gideon took to their own spots, waiting for Aaron's count.

Anthony played, holding his breath for when the women came in. He knew they were professionals but hearing his bandmates — who'd been musicians all their lives — made him nervous.

Gideon hit the emotional center of the song, and Anthony took a deep breath. When the women came in, soft and slow, an echo of Gideon's own sadness, Anthony felt silly for worrying. He finished his part, the women finished theirs, and Gideon ended the piece. Anthony looked at his comrades. They looked as excited as he felt, and Tom's words of encouragement only ballooned the feeling. Aaron and Nate talked about something before Aaron came over the speaker, asking the women to harmonize a touch more to give it an almost gospel sound.

"Dude." Anthony turned to Gideon, excited. "This links so well to the last song on our first album."

"*Divinity*?"

"Yeah."

"But we can't open our new album with a ballad."

Anthony looked at his cousin. "I mean... Why not?"

"Because it's a ballad. We need something more upbeat." Gideon shook his head. "I thought we were opening with *Lavender* since it's sax heavy, like *Divinity*."

"But *Lavender* is soft. Not ballad soft, but soft. I think opening with a ballad would actually be a cool change to the standard album release."

"Hey guys?" Tom came over the speaker. "This is a great discussion that we should all be in on, so let's shelve the convo and record the changes, yeah?"

"Yep," Anthony and Gideon said in unison, returning to their stations.

Aaron counted them in, the song second nature to Anthony as he waited for the women's voices to join Gideon's.

And when they did, they were as heavenly as Nate had asked for, and as heavenly as the song needed for justice to be done.

22

The delirium Julie felt navigating the subways of New York City after over twenty-four hours of traveling across the world was like nothing she'd ever experienced before.

Everything was so loud, so gray, in comparison to her little streets in the Himalayas. There was no rushing Ganga, no mooing cows, no neighborly calls in the street. Instead, everyone wore headphones and threw annoyed glances at one another for being too slow, too fast, too loud, too quiet. No one smiled.

She exited the subway in her old neighborhood, walking the broad Upper West Side streets to the apartment she shared with Rachel, Ben, and Ella, before she moved in with Gideon. It was one of Rachel's family's apartments but, for the time being, her dad allowed them to live there rent free. She stopped in front of the building, just now realizing how nice of a building it was. When she pulled open the doors, she was greeted by a new front deskman. Julie wasn't in the mood to chat or be questioned as to why a grimy backpacker was entering the premise, so she waved her front door key so he knew she belonged.

The elevator was faster than she remembered, an almost sad change from the stairs she'd grown used to climbing to reach her room. When it dinged open, she stepped into the hallway, almost forgetting which door was hers.

It'd been so long.

Her roommates knew she'd be home today, but not what time. Thankfully, it was only early afternoon in the middle of the week. Julie opened the door to the plush apartment, hesitantly walking down the hall to her bedroom. To have a place like India feel like home, only to return to the place that bore the title and have it not feel how it used to…

Julie sat on her bed and unclipped her backpack from her hips and chest. Pushing it off the bed, she laid back on the down comforter.

It wasn't that this place didn't feel like home. It just didn't feel *as* home as her bare hotel room, or that cavernous tutoring room. Her heart panged with the tearful goodbye she'd had with her students. Her and Akhila promised to be pen pals. Sanjay had brought her a marigold, a humble flower currently pressed between the pages of a book taken from the hotel's lending library shelf. Kat had given her a tight hug. A motherly hug.

Julie sat up. Now that she was back, she'd have to mend some of the relationships she'd broken before she'd left. She'd told her dad in August that she was leaving in September, but she hadn't told him when she was coming back. She sent him a quick text saying she was stateside and exhausted.

She needed a shower.

Water had never felt so good, but exiting the warmth of the bathroom resulted in a barrage of aches and pains. Other than her quick stop in Goa, Julie had been going virtually nonstop since she boarded her first international flight in the fall. Now she was met with a tsunami of exhaustion and a mind that was too wired to sleep.

Laying in bed, staring at the ceiling, Julie was weighing the need to reset with the need to get her life here started. She'd speak with Rachel and Ella later in the week about how Maven Media could expand into a nonprofit, and what that nonprofit would do. She'd speak on the phone with her dad, see what could be done about her failed relationship with her mom. She'd avoid Ruby at all costs.

And Anthony.

Julie clenched her eyes, trying to push his Tom Cruise smile and broad shoulders and homemade enchiladas from her mind. Traveling had enabled her to focus on herself, which was something she'd never apologize for. Even if he was a casualty of that war. It had provided distractions and insight. It had given her a space to grieve and understand why she allowed him to get close to her while knowing she really wasn't as emotionally available as he deserved.

She had foolishly thought they were each broken enough to make a whole.

They hadn't spoken since that morning so long ago, when she told him it'd been a mistake. That they'd been a mistake. She knew she'd have to at some point. But Julie didn't know what she wanted from the conversation.

He was probably seeing Ruby by now. He'd probably never trust Julie with his heart again. She knew, even after all this distance, that she still loved him as fiercely as she once had.

Maybe that love would be enough.

23

Anthony grabbed two Coca-Colas, pouring the soda over ice in the kitchen while he watched Gideon on the couch. They needed to talk about their fight, clear the air. It'd been long enough. Once they did that, maybe Anthony would have the courage to tell Gideon about his mom.

He brought the glasses over, plopping down on the cushion beside his cousin.

It was now or never,

"So, Gid. I know things seem fine, but I wanted to clear the air."

Gideon sipped his drink, avoiding Anthony's gaze. "There's not much to clear. I don't think it was a good idea to get involved with Ruby. You got involved with Ruby. Now Julie's back."

The room became cold, Anthony's heart freezing.

"What did you say?"

"You didn't know?" Gideon looked at Anthony, shocked. "Yeah, she came home a few days ago."

The world felt like it was spinning too fast and not fast enough. Anthony set his drink on the coffee table.

"She's back?"

"She's back." Gideon shook his head. "Anthony, we're practically brothers. I'll always be there for you. There's just nothing I can really do in this situation, and that sucks. Are things serious with Ruby?"

Anthony stared at a dent in the old coffee table, trying to sort his thoughts. "No, we agreed to keep things casual. It's more of like... friends with benefits? We just end up having a good time. And we've only slept together a couple of times."

After seeing each other for a month, they'd slipped into that territory. Anthony had tried to kick the guilty feeling and had finally started to enjoy the intimacy of another person. For years, he was able to slip from woman to woman, brunettes to blondes to redheads. That all changed when he opened himself to Julie. He used to think he never wanted to be that person again.

Now he couldn't be that person fast enough.

"Well, from what Ella's said, Julie might be going back to work at Maven Media. So just... prepare yourself. It's going to be messy."

"Messy for who, Gideon? Julie broke my heart. I've moved on." Anthony looked at his cousin, trying to ignore the metallic taste of the half-lie. "If she has a problem with me seeing someone she happens to know, but someone that I do genuinely like, that's not really my problem."

Gideon sighed. "But it is a problem, Ant. They work together. I'm engaged to Ella and they do publicity for our band. Which means our circles are linked for the foreseeable future."

"So? It'll be awkward until Julie gets over it. Besides, Ruby and I are casual. Just seeing how things go. And as far as I'm concerned, this is Julie's hurdle. She fucked up." Anthony felt his heart start to race at the made-up thought of Julie having an issue with him moving on. At the made-up thought that maybe — just maybe — she'd fight for him and what they once shared.

"I just want you to be honest with yourself. You're pretending to be over someone that fucked you up."

"Like you did with Ella?" Anthony hadn't meant to throw his cousin's once-complicated relationship in his face. Gideon's issues with alcohol had come between him and Ella a few times, once even with Anthony's help. "You seemed to work it out."

"Ella didn't string me along." Gideon's voice was calm, his eyes steely as he stared at Anthony. Anthony couldn't quite shake the feeling he was speaking to a disappointed parent.

"So Ella can forgive you for being an alcoholic but I can't forgive Julie for ditching me to figure herself out — after she's already forgiven me for dropping her like a stone in the sea for my addiction? Doesn't make sense, Gideon."

"I just want you to be honest with yourself, man. For months, you've gone on about how she broke your heart and you never want to see her again. I've never believed it, and then you find comfort in the arms of one of her coworkers. But now you're getting all amped up and talking like you'd take Julie back if she still wanted you. So what do you want, Anthony?" Gideon slammed his empty glass on the coffee table and stood. "Once you've figured it out, let me know." He grabbed his jacket and stormed out of the apartment.

Anthony laughed at how ridiculous and right Gideon was. Standing, pacing the living room, he thought about what Gideon said.

Julie was the only woman he'd ever loved. She was the only woman he could ever imagine spending his life with.

Yeah, if Julie still wanted him, if she could earn his trust back, he would take her back.

He had been pushing, straining himself, to believe that it wasn't true. He feared the judgement of everyone around him. He feared she'd break him all over again.

But he also knew there was no one that made him feel the way Julie did.

24

Looking in the full-length mirror, Julie smoothed her sheath dress and turned to check out her heels. As much as she'd missed her slew of fashionable clothes while traveling, now that she was constricted in them, she missed her yoga pants and loose tunics.

The din from the cafe could be heard through the closed door, and Julie was thankful she'd arrived early for her formal meeting with Rachel and Ella. She was able to save them a table and redo her lipstick. She'd done market research and typed up a proposal for a nonprofit that could be built under Maven Media. Despite working for them in the past, Julie wanted to show them she could still be the professional she'd been before she dropped everything.

Except for having the meeting at the Maven Media office; she didn't trust herself to be professional with that.

When she'd asked Rachel and Ella if they could meet at a cafe instead, they'd shared a look that further instilled fear in her heart. Julie hadn't had the bandwidth or the courage to ask about Ruby. She'd come home from India, slept for two days, and immediately dove into her nonprofit work. One weeknight she spent relaxing with her three best friends, getting caught up on everything she'd missed.

Now it was time to go back to the boss bitch she'd always been.

When she returned to the table, Julie was greeted with hugs from Rachel and Ella. She sat across from them, taking in their pristine make-up and chic blouses. She'd missed working. She'd missed bouncing ideas off of people. She'd missed researching.

"It's so nice to have you back, Jules." Ella released a heavy sigh, laying across the table. Julie laughed, immediately feeling at home.

"Truly. We have as much time as we need for this, but let's get the business over with so we can hang out at this 'business lunch.'" Rachel smiled and nodded toward the stack of papers in front of Julie.

Julie pulled out two bound booklets, containing the printed slides of a presentation she'd made, and passed one to Rachel and one to Ella. She had loose pages of her various notes and talking points at the ready.

"I was fortunate to have the experience of volunteering at a home in the mountains of Northern India. The home — which housed seventy kids between the ages of newborn to thirteen — also provided schooling to these children and over a hundred other children in the area, deemed at risk. This nonprofit focused on rescuing children and their mothers from poverty and abusive situations, to give them a second chance at life and an avenue to escape the vicious cycle they're born into." Julie watched her friends' faces fall while they flipped through the booklet, armed with the horrific data of prostitution, child labor, and domestic abuse.

She cleared her throat. "Given Maven Media's strong foundation as a business that seeks to amplify the voices of women and marginalized communities, it would be instrumental in the company's growth to place energy into a nonprofit sector that focuses on the very thing its founded on. I propose the nonprofit focuses on rehabilitating domestic abuse survivors, providing child care to those of single parents, and after school programs for at-risk youth. These after school programs could focus not just on tutoring, but on the arts. That will help tie it into the markets Maven Media works in. The first year, we would focus on building awareness, finding donors, and receiving licenses for tutoring, child care, and shelter. The second year, we would invest in a space and outfit it to house, tutor, and provide child care."

"What's the competition like?" Rachel's espresso eyes, all business, pierced Julie's.

"There are a variety of programs for each individual need, but not one that offers all that we'd offer. And there's no publicity company that has a nonprofit branch. Which helps set us apart from other companies."

Ella nodded, pursing her lips. "How would we help those that come to us from falling back into the hole they'd gotten out of?"

"I was thinking we could eventually add classes for the women. Financial advisement, self-care, stress management, healthy mindsets."

"Maybe year three we could set up a section of the nonprofit where, upon an application and interview, we financially take care of a single-parent family for a finite period of time," Rachel added. "We could have volunteer counselors or something who help develop individualized plans for the families to get back on their feet. They could meet every week or month to make sure everything's on track and adjust accordingly."

Julie swallowed the lump in her throat. She couldn't imagine the reach, the good, this program could do. Maven Media was the perfect vehicle to spread the word. She thought of all the women she'd met, all the children, who just needed a little help. Who needed a clean slate or a second chance. She thought of Hannah, her sister, whose death sent her parents into a depressed spiral and left Julie, a seventeen-year-old, to pick up the pieces. She'd managed — she was privileged — but there were so many others who couldn't. There were others who, like her, had family that had disowned them.

The past year had brought Julie face-to-face with herself, and she'd seen what guilt and shame could do to a person. She saw the walls untouched emotions could build, and how those walls eventually grew so tall you became lost behind them, or fell to crush whoever was trying to find you.

25

Anthony sat on the couch in Gideon and Ella's apartment, mulling over his cousin's advice. Gideon was the king of mending broken relationships — surely he'd know how Anthony should approach reconnecting with his mom. And it sounded like Gideon did know. Go slow, don't expect anything. Anthony would never have the parent he wanted or deserved; he just had whatever that parent could give.

It would just help if she would respond to his last message.

In person. Mom.

Maybe her new family was too awesome and distracting and she'd forgotten.

"Ant, it's going to be okay." Gideon gave him a half-smile before shoving a handful of Doritos in his mouth. "I'm sure she's just as nervous to see you, if not more. I mean, she completely dipped out on her family."

"Yeah. Yeah, you're probably right. I kind of just want to get it over with, you know? I feel like she dangled a carrot in front of me and I can't stop thinking about it."

"Makes sense. But there's nothing you can do but what I told you. Easier said than done, I know."

"Yeah. Thanks again, I think I'm gonna head out." Anthony stood, needing space more than anything. Gideon stood and gave him a tight hug.

"Keep me posted on what happens, Ant."

"Of course. Tell Ella I say hey."

Anthony let himself out, trying not to hold onto the idea that Ella was probably out with Julie, and that at some point, he'd have to run into Julie, with nothing to say.

"Anthony?"

Speak of the fucking devil.

"Hey, Ella." Anthony was mildly startled to see her until he realized he was still on her block, standing in front of the corner deli. Thankfully, she was alone. "How's it going?"

She peered into the store before turning to Anthony. "It's going. Yeah, you know, it's good." Ella gave a nervous laugh that turned Anthony's spine stiff.

"Ella, what's — "

The deli door opened, a laughing Julie saying something to the man behind the counter, her head turned, her arms carrying three pints of ice cream. She bumped into Ella, who reached out an arm to stabilize her friend before the ice cream hit the concrete. But there was nothing Ella could do about the way Julie's jaw dropped when she saw Anthony.

And there was nothing Anthony wanted to do more than stare into her ocean depths, and spend every minute relearning her mouth while she took him back.

"So... I'm gonna take that ice cream, Jules. Buzz up when you get there." Ella scrambled to take the ice cream from Julie before awkwardly dipping out of the conversation.

A conversation Anthony still didn't have the words for.

He shoved his hands in his pockets, rocking from ball to heel. Trying to find what was different and what had stayed the same. Her golden skin had burned even deeper, her blond locks longer and brighter than they'd been. She seemed slimmer, her curves not as pronounced, but her face felt more open than it ever had. Like she knew everything about him already, and she wasn't there to judge. Like she just wanted to be there, beside him or anyone else, for the sake of being beside them.

"Wow." Julie shook her head. "I'm — I'm sorry, I'm speechless. I wasn't expecting to see you."

Anthony forced a chuckle. "You mean you don't normally run into an ex on your best friend's street trying not to drop a gallon of ice cream?"

A soft breath left her lips, passing as a laugh. "You know me. Can never have too much ice cream." Julie titled her head. Eyes bright, she gave him a genuine smile.

No matter how small it was, he'd take it.

"It's good to see you, Anthony. We should catch up. Properly." Her smile fell as she hugged herself, averting her gaze to the bubble-gummed sidewalk.

Anthony swallowed and looked around on the off chance she looked back at him.

"Yeah, sure. You have my number." He cleared his throat, risking a glance at her.

Those blue eyes looked at him, carrying ocean currents and lost summer skies. He felt himself start to unravel at the hidden words, the memories set just below the skin.

"Yeah, I do. I'll reach out." She gave a sad smile

before pushing past him, the familiar scent of vanilla and rose rising from the passing curls of her hair. He turned, desperate to see her. Desperate to know she was real.

Desperate to know if she would turn to look at him.

She climbed the stoop leading to the apartment and pressed the buzzer. And turned to face Anthony before pulling the door open and disappearing.

26

Julie burst through the building door and leaned against the stair railing, trying to catch her breath. Trying to stop the tearing in her heart at the sight of him.

Anthony looked better than she remembered. Broad shoulders, clean-shaven, shortish dark hair. An ache behind the eyes she knew she was responsible for. When she brushed past him — hopelessly trying to be near his strength and warmth once more — he still smelled of the warm ginger and citrus she'd always loved.

Starting up the stairs, Julie tried to decipher how he felt towards her; the walls she'd been able to help him tear down last year were firmly reconstructed.

He was just friendly enough to make her think there might be hope but just guarded enough to wonder if it was worth trying.

Her heart tore a little more at the thought.

For him, it would always be worth trying.

The door to Ella and Gideon's apartment stood ajar, and Julie let herself in. She followed the trail of their low voices to the living room, where they were snuggled on the sleep black sofa. Ella popped up from Gideon's chest, tossing the fluffy throw to the side.

"Honey, are you okay?" Ella stepped forward, cautiously, an arm outstretched in case Julie needed someone to catch her if she fell.

Julie nodded, blinking back tears. She had no right to cry. She'd pushed him away and, seven months later, he was seeing someone else. She had no right to feel this strange claim on him.

But none of that mattered in the face of a broken heart, and she couldn't keep the tears at bay for long. She buried her face in Ella's shoulder, the replacement mom-hug she so desperately needed after all of these months. Ella rocked her, squeezed her, let her sob until her shirt was soaked.

Eventually the sobs subsided, and Julie pulled

back from her best friend, her family. She wiped her eyes, a momentary embarrassment at losing her cool in front of Gideon. He may have been engaged to Ella, but he was still Anthony's cousin. But Gideon had left the room.

"Come sit, Jules." Ella grabbed her hand, leading her to the sofa. "Gideon's making tea — I told him it's the cure-all for you."

Ella settled in the corner, pulling Julie into her side. They stayed that way until Gideon came in with lavender, peppermint, and chamomile wafting from three steaming mugs.

"Here you go. I'll leave you two to it." Gideon set two of the mugs down before grabbing his own.

Traveling by herself had strengthened Julie's inherent sense of independence. But it also taught her that it was okay to ask for help. Julie sniffled. "No, no. It's okay. You probably know more about everything than Ella, and I could just... use some help."

"If you're sure." He sat on her other side and patted her back before turning his attention to the mug in his hand.

"What happened?" Ella still held Julie's hand and gave it a small squeeze.

"Nothing. Literally. We said hi. I said we should catch up. He said I knew how to reach him. I said I would and left." She started crying again, but not until after she caught the glance between Ella and Gideon.

"Well, what did you expect to happen?" Gideon's voice was calm, nonjudgmental. Ella had always talked about how kind he was in serious situations, and she was thankful her friend hadn't just imagined it.

"I don't know." Julie wiped her nose on her sleeve. "I just thought maybe he'd be excited to see me. Or I'd be excited to see him. And I wasn't. It just... hurt."

"Jules, you know why he wouldn't be excited to see you, right?"

"Yeah, every reason. It was a surprise. Ruby. He's still hurt about everything. Or he doesn't care enough to feel any sort of way."

Gideon's laugh was strained. "I promise you, it's not because he doesn't care. The guy's completely sick over what to do."

Julie looked at him, the man that resembled Anthony. The cousins were both tall, broad, black haired with blue eyes. But Gideon was sharper, harder, more brooding. Anthony was gentler, softer, more open.

"Isn't — isn't he seeing Ruby, though?" Julie tried to keep down the crack in her voice.

"Look, you need to talk to him. I'm just saying he doesn't know what he wants but if I had to place bets, I'd say he's still hung up on you."

27

"Hey, you." Ruby raised up on her tip toes and pressed her lips against Anthony's.

"Hey." He pressed back, feeling the velvet slip of her tongue between his teeth before she pulled away. Her eyes were cool as she pushed past him into his apartment. He closed the door and wiped his mouth with the back of his hand in case there was a smear of red lipstick. He followed her into the kitchen, watching her slim hips in cropped jeans. Her hair was pulled into a curly ponytail tied with a patterned scarf, a drapey white shirt beneath her favorite leather jacket.

Ruby grabbed a glass of water, watching him over the rim as she drank.

"How are you?" Anthony leaned against the

island. They hadn't seen each other in a bit, and he'd felt the familiar ache of missing someone.

Missing someone he probably shouldn't, which only made matters worse.

"Great." She set down her glass and crossed her arms. "How about you?"

"Good. Busy, the band finally wrapped up recording the second album. What have you been up to?"

She narrowed her eyes at him. "Anthony, do us both a favor and just be honest. I'm not here for games."

He shifted his gaze, mentally kicking himself. Of course Ruby would pick up on his distance — she had to know Julie was back, and she had to know he would know. He thought over the last few days he'd been able to hide how rattled he was after running into Julie.

Guess not.

Ruby was right. She'd always been a straight shooter with him, and she deserved at least as much from him.

"You're right." Anthony sighed and met her eyes. Hazel, this time, ringed with blue. "I've been feeling a bit distant, and I'm sorry."

"Julie?"

"I... I think so. I know we said we'd keep things casual, you and I. And I don't really want to talk to her right now. But it is weird when you've been able to kind of convince yourself someone you loved no longer existed, and then... they come back."

"Seriously?" Ruby barked out a laugh. "Look, I know we said we'd keep things casual, but it's been a couple of months. If you're still hung up on your ex, I'm out. You know?"

"Yeah, I know. But — "

"But you don't want to 'lose' me?" Ruby air-quoted. "Anthony, c'mon. You're a grown ass man."

Anthony took a step back, surprised by her sudden fire. "Ruby, we agreed to be casual. You knew I was still getting over someone. And you could've been seeing other people or getting over someone yourself. That's the whole point of casual."

"Well, maybe I wanted something more."

"Well, maybe you shouldn't be putting that on me when you didn't even tell me."

They stood there, breathing heavy. Anthony felt the heat in his cheeks probably matched the color in hers. Somehow, hearing she didn't just want to be casual gave him pause. He set his hands on his hips, trying to think through how to move forward.

"What do you want, Anthony?" The fight had left her voice, her shoulders sagging.

"I don't know."

"Okay. I'm not waiting around while you figure it out. I wish you luck, with whatever it ends up being." She shrugged her shoulders and headed toward the front door. Anthony could do nothing more than helplessly walk behind her, mumbling an "I'm sorry" to her back as she refused to turn around. He waited until she was out of the building hallway to shut the door, softly.

Left alone in the apartment once more, Anthony ambled back into the living room and looked around.

What did he want?

He'd already admitted to Gideon — and himself — that at the end of the day it would always be Julie. But he didn't know what to say to her right now, especially not after putting the ball in her court when they ran into each other on the street. He already missed Ruby's sweetness, the way she laughed at everything even when it wasn't funny.

But did he?

Anthony realized he was slipping into his old habit of drowning himself in someone, something, to avoid facing reality. It used to be women and alcohol, before the car accident. It used to be drugs, before rehab. It used to be Julie, who had shown him what it meant to love someone unconditionally. Even when that someone had no idea what they were doing.

28

Ben looked at Julie, expectant.

"So, are you going to do it? Call Anthony?"

Julie turned from her roommate and toward the TV, pretending to focus on the cartoon show they both loved. Anything to put off that phone call.

"Jules."

She sighed and swung her head towards Ben, resting it on the back of the couch while she looked at him. Her friend had cut the floppy gingerbread hair he'd had since she met him through Ella in college. The short sides and longer top made him look more adult, though his large eyes were now more pronounced. Startling, in a handsome kind of way. She swung her head back to the TV.

"Yeah, dad. I'm going to call him. Tomorrow."

"Why are you putting it off?" Ben had always been the voice of reason in their friend group, and that had only gotten worse as they'd gotten older.

"Because he can wait another a day."

He laughed. "Fair. What are you going to say? Are you nervous?"

"Oh, please." Julie rolled her eyes. If nothing else, an attempt to seem as apathetic as possible. "I'm just going to say we should meet. I was thinking a nice coffee shop or something."

Ben cocked his head. "You really want to have that convo in a public place?"

"You really think he and I should be alone in one of our apartments?" Julie raised an eyebrow. "It's too personal."

"Too intimate," Ben corrected.

Julie chewed her lip. The chemistry between her and Anthony had always felt like an inferno. An everlasting fire. She could be wrong — she could've done more damage than she realized — but she doubted any length of time could diminish those flames. But she knew nothing would happen between them that first meeting. She just didn't want to be in his apartment, surrounded by the things that looked and smelled like him when she couldn't have him. And she didn't want to put him through that by having him in her space.

"Jules, what are you actually going to say to him? When you meet?"

"Ben, you know it depends on what he says." Julie really wanted this conversation to stop. She knew everything out of Ben's mouth would show the glaring holes in her plan. It was a loose plan, for sure, but it was the only semblance of order and control that she had in the situation. It was the only semblance of order and control she had in her life at all while she waited for Ella and Rachel to iron out the nonprofit details and rehire her.

"Just tell me your options, your thoughts." He stood and headed into the kitchen. "Want some chips?"

"Yeah, salt and vinegar, please." The cartoon episode was actually pretty funny, the kids whose dad runs a burger joint having to run around finding the person who stole everyone's Halloween candy. The slight distraction was made even better when Ben handed her the bag of requested chips. They sat in silence for a moment, munching.

"Well, I kind of want to see where he stands first," Julie said, breaking the silence. "I need to know if it's too late, and if not, how close I am to him walking away for good. If it's not too late, I still need to know where his head's at. Does he want space? Does he want to try the friends route first or just pick up where we left off?"

Ben nodded, eyes trained on the show. "And what if it is too late?"

Julie swallowed the lump in her throat. She'd had lots of practice imagining those would be his words. So why did it hurt so much?

"If he says it's too late... I'm still going to fight. It'll hurt deeper. It'll take longer. But he's my person." She released the breath she'd been holding, the words weighted with truth. From her periphery she saw Ben glance at her before turning back to the show.

"Good," he said. "Love is always worth fighting for."

29

Anthony sat at the island, watching his dad cook them spaghetti. It was coming up on a year since Anthony had been checked into rehab, a little less since Tom had bought the small apartment in New York City for Anthony to recover in while he took off for Eternal Youths' summer festival tour. While their relationship went from being thick as thieves when Anthony was growing up to being tense while he moved through college, they'd been able to find a comfortable silence in living together since Anthony's recovery.

"Hey bud, could you grab me some more paper towels?"

Anthony jumped up and headed to the restroom, where they stored extra paper products. He came back bearing an extra roll, stopping in his tracks at his dad leaning over the island, sauce abandoned on the stove.

"Dad?"

Tom straightened but didn't look at Anthony. Anthony looked at the black countertop, seeing the reflection of the overhead light in his phone.

Why was his dad looking at Anthony's phone?

"Dad, here are the paper towels." Anthony moved cautiously forward, his father still not looking at or answering him. Anthony set the new roll on the island. "Did something happen?"

Tom turned to the sauce. Anthony could hear the bubbling and knew it needed to be stirred, but his dad just stared at it. Anthony picked up the phone, the culprit.

A message from Christine Scott, asking if next week was okay to meet.

The air stilled around Anthony. Without saying so, his dad had made it clear not to reach out to his mom. It didn't matter that she spent eighteen years loving them and then vanished without saying so much as a goodbye. It didn't matter that she never returned any of Anthony's calls or texts. It didn't matter that Tom had told Anthony about his mom's alcoholic tendencies last year.

It didn't matter, because Tom was still hurting.

Anthony watched his dad, eyes scrunched and hands white-knuckling the oven handle. He was immediately transported to being a kid, probably around the age of eight, and his dad being so upset about something Anthony had done that he just walked out of the room, leaving the punishment to his mom.

Tom faced his son, face red. "Why? She ABANDONED us." The controlled anger of his words caused Anthony to flinch.

His dad didn't yell. Ever.

"Anthony." Tom lowered his head, breathed. Collected himself. "I told you what you needed to know. She didn't want us anymore. That's why she left. Why would you talk to her?" When he looked up, Anthony saw tears collecting in his eyes.

Anthony shifted his weight, feeling all of eighteen when he realized his mom had left. When he'd come down the stairs from his room and saw his dad sitting at the kitchen table, staring out the window. His mom's car was gone, and her favorite coat. But it was the empty slivers in the bookcase that made it all click in Anthony's head. She'd never leave her books.

But she'd leave her family.

"I needed to know why, dad. You got the closure of a divorce. I just had a mom that up and left."

He felt small, saying the words he'd held onto for so long. He hadn't even needed to tell Gideon — his cousin just knew.

Tom nodded. "Okay. I don't want to know anything about her or what she has to say." He untied his apron, setting it on the island before leaving the room. Anthony watched him shuffle down the hallway to his room, seeming years older than his late fifties would suggest.

The sauce still boiled on the stove, accompanied by the acrid smell of burnt tomatoes and the feeling Anthony continued to find in this apartment of being impossibly alone.

30

Julie paced the kitchen, tapping her phone against her hand. It was just a phone call, and there was a high probability it would end in a voicemail.

She knew she just needed to call Anthony and see where they stood. Once she knew, she could move forward. She thought back to all the times in India where she knew she needed to let things go. That if it was meant to be, it would be. But she also knew things rarely fell into your lap, and there usually had to be some work done to get the desired chain of events.

So she just needed to call.

Deep breath. Deep breath.

"Hey."

His voice was rough on the other end, and her

breath caught. Julie had fully expected it to go to voicemail.

"Julie?"

Oh, god. Even the way he said her name undid her. Slow, like he was tasting every letter. Like how he used to taste her.

"Hey, Anthony." She cleared her throat, trying to find something to say. "I told you I'd reach out."

"You did. I mean, you're a lawyer so I'm not surprised you followed through."

She bit her nail through her smile, unsure of how to speak the words lodged in her throat. The sooner she did it, the sooner it would be over.

"So... We should talk." *Too serious.* "Chat." *Better.* "Catch up."

He chuckled. "All three?"

"If you're up for it." She smiled at his willingness to banter. "I was thinking we should meet at a coffee shop or cafe or something?"

Julie waited through his silence, listening to his gentle breathing on the other end.

"You don't think it would be better somewhere more... private?"

Her breath hitched at his suggestion. The same one Ben had thrown at her. But it was a hell of a lot easier explaining to Ben how she didn't want to be with Anthony in an intimate setting. Not when they had a track record of off-the-charts chemistry. It was a risk she wasn't sure she wanted to take, not until she knew more about his relationship with Ruby.

"I didn't know if that would be... uncomfortable for you," she said.

More silence. More nail chewing. She wouldn't have fingers left by the time they were through.

Anthony sighed. "I know what you mean, but I think I'd rather be uncomfortable in private than in public."

"Okay. Have a place in mind?" Julie hoped he'd say her place; at least then she'd be in her territory. But the longer he was silent, the more she thought. "Do you know of maybe a third-party space? Not yours or mine?"

"Actually... I could ask Gideon or Ella if maybe we could use their apartment? Or would that be weirder than one of our places?"

"I don't think it's any weirder. There aren't as many memories, you know?"

"Yeah." His voice was soft, and Julie yearned to be close to him. She let the admission hang between them, not ready to hang up the phone or pick a day.

Anthony beat her to it. "How does this weekend sound?"

"That works. I guess we can see what works for Ella and Gideon and move forward from there?"

"Sure. I... I really want to hear about your travels."

She smiled. He'd always asked her questions — it used to be too much, back before she realized the only way to love someone was to let them in. But he was still curious about her and she would hold onto that, even if she shouldn't. Even if there was the possibility she was reading too much into it.

"I want to hear about the new music." *And your recovery. And Ruby.*

Anthony didn't respond. Julie thought maybe the call had dropped until she heard him breathing.

"Is the music okay?" she asked.

"Oh, yeah. Sorry." He sighed. "Actually, the music is fine but I... I got a message from my mom."

Julie froze. "What did she want, Anthony?"

"She agreed to meet with me. Next week."

She knew what this meant to him, knew that this would finally provide the closure he'd been craving since he was a teen. It'd been the reason why he was so closed off to those that he met, especially romantic interests.

"That's good, Anthony. I'm happy for you. Whatever comes of it, you'll get exactly what you need."

"Thanks. Yeah, that's a nice way of looking at it. I knew you'd understand."

Julie could hear the smile in his voice, a bridge between who they were before and who they were now.

31

Anthony laid in bed, waiting for Julie to say something.

He wanted her to know he wasn't completely shutting down the idea of reconnecting. He wanted her to know that, despite rebuilding some of the walls she'd taken down, he could trust her as a friend.

"Are you nervous?"

Her voice was soft, feeling a world away from where he wanted her to be.

"For sure." Anthony smoothed the comforter, playing with the seam on his sheets. "I don't know what she'll be like. I know she has two daughters, but I don't know anything about them. I might have sisters. I don't know if she'll tell me what I want to hear or what I already know."

He listened to some soft padding, the creak of a door, the rustle of her own sheets.

"What do you want her to say?" she asked.

The plop of a curvy blonde turning over in bed, clutching the phone so it wouldn't drop. So she wouldn't miss a word.

"I want her to be honest. Even if it's true she didn't want me and my dad anymore, that's okay. But if she loved us, I'd like to know that, too." Anthony took a deep breath. "How are things with your parents?"

Julie laughed. "Oh, please. Haven't spoken to my mom since the fight in July. I've reached out a couple of times to my dad to let him know I'm alive and well."

Anthony thought back to last summer, when she'd had to return home to Chicago for the tenth anniversary of the car accident that had claimed her younger sister. Julie had been driving when someone else ran a red and crashed into the passenger side. But the light Julie went through had been yellow, and her mother was never able to move past her belief that Julie should have just stopped.

He ran his fingers through his hair, searching for

his own reminder. The scar was a symbol, a consequence, of his drunk stupidity. He'd been the only one hurt, but it had killed his ability to walk and play music, and had led to substance abuse.

Which led to rehab and reconnecting with Julie.

"Do you ever think about these horrible things that happen, but if they hadn't happened, you wouldn't be exactly where you are?" he asked.

"Of course," she breathed into the phone. "I used to hate it. Like, why did I have to be right here, right now? Why couldn't I just have my younger sister and a mom that loved me and a life I loved?"

"What changed?"

"I wasn't happy, so something had to change."

Anthony picked at the thread on the sheet. "Is that why you took off?"

Her sigh on the other end was a summer breeze. "Yes. I needed perspective. To get out of my head in some ways and deeper into it in others."

"Are you happy with where you are?"

"For the most part. I'm happier than I've been in years. I feel like I have a purpose. I feel sure of myself in a way that's bone deep, not skin deep. Still missing a few things, but that's okay." Julie paused, her breath quickening. "Are — are you happy with where you are?"

He thought about what she said. He was happiest last summer, when they spent hot days walking around New York City. When she'd been a shoulder for him to lean on post-rehab, and he'd shown her it was okay to let your guard down. Before that, his happiness was skin deep: frontman for a popular band, parties every weekend, girls whenever he wanted. After... After, he knew what it felt like to wake up in the morning, thankful to be waking up. He knew what it was like to be supported by the ones he loved. He knew what it felt like to have the sun kiss his skin, the trail of her blonde hair against his arm. He knew what it was like to worship the sun.

"Yes, I am."

"Good." He heard the lilt in her response, knew she had a smile playing at the corners of her lips. "I'm getting sleepy, Anthony. Thanks for chatting. And if you need anything, I'm here for you."

"Likewise. Have sweet dreams, Julie."

He hung up but held the phone to his chest, wishing it smelled of vanilla and rose.

32

"Are you sure you can skip going into the office?" Julie looked at Ella over the rim of her mug. They were seated on opposite ends of the couch, the apartment empty of Rachel and Ben.

"Yes. You know how it is there, Rachel doesn't really care when you come in as long as the work gets done." Ella sipped her coffee. "What did you want to talk about?"

Julie cradled the hot mug. "I spoke to Anthony last night."

"Oh, really?" Ella perked up, causing Julie to smile. She'd missed her best friend's enthusiasm.

"Yeah. We were thinking of meeting maybe next week."

"Before or after he meets his mom?"

Julie jerked. "Oh, I didn't know you knew about that. Actually, we wanted to ask you guys if we could use your apartment to talk. You know, it's not as... intimate, as meeting in one of ours."

Ella cocked her head. "That kind of feels like bullshit, Jules. We're adults, we've had hard conversations in places we haven't wanted to. I think you should just have him come here. Plan it for a Sunday when Rachel's with her family and Ben's at his boothang's."

"I guess." Julie bit her lower lip. "I just want it to be as easy as possible."

"Ha! Girl, you know it doesn't matter *where* you talk. Just do it. You should probably meet with him a day or two after after he sees his mom, he'll need a friend other than Gideon."

"He doesn't want to talk to Ruby?" Julie couldn't keep the bitterness from sliding into the words.

"As far as I know, they haven't seen each other in awhile." Ella focused on her coffee. "Ruby and I aren't great friends — I am technically her boss, and she knows you and I are best friends — but I haven't heard anything through the grapevine, from her or from Gideon."

"Hmmm." Julie pursed her lips. "When we get

the nonprofit stuff sorted, will I have to work in the office?"

Ella set her mug on the coffee table, angling herself to face Julie. Her green eyes bore into Julie. "Yeah, you will. I'm sorry, there's just no real way around it. You don't know the extent of their relationship, so try not to work yourself up too much."

"You're right. I know you're right." Julie rested her head in her hand, her brain spinning with all the things Anthony and Ruby could have possibly done and felt.

"Speaking of, we're meeting with Maven Media's corporate lawyers about the nonprofit branch this week. So we'll know more about your status by next week."

Julie looked at her beaming friend and couldn't stop her own smile from growing. One of her favorite things about Ella was how fast she was at doing whatever it was she said she'd do.

"Thank you so much for this."

"I'm so excited to make this part of our company, Jules." Ella sobered, picking her mug back up but not drinking from it. "Was it Hannah? That made you want to volunteer?"

Julie looked away, remembering her sister with long dirty blonde hair and rosy cheeks. Freckled arms and brown eyes, a snort that passed as a laugh.

"I guess in a way. In India, I met a man who sponsored one of the children at the orphanage. He had this... sense of calm about him. I never learned this name, but everything he said felt like it clicked into place. I had to see what helped make him like that. I visited and fell in love."

"With whom?"

Julie laughed with her friend. "The kids. All of them. I helped ten second graders and five eighth graders. But Sanjay and Akhila..." She wiped the tears from her cheeks. "Sorry, I don't know why I've been getting so emotional lately."

Ella patted Julie's arm. "Nothing to be sorry for. There's a lot to feel. These kids must've really meant something to you."

Julie nodded. Sanjay had big brown eyes, like Hannah had. His chubby hands always found a piece of Julie to hold, his mop of dark hair almost always sticking up in odd directions. He was missing a couple teeth, the gaps solidifying that no matter how old he seemed, he was still only seven. She hadn't been there long, but she'd been able to see what a difference that kind of love and attention made.

She wondered what it'd be like to help them a little longer. A little more permanently.

"What are you thinking about, Jules?" Ella's voice cut through the realization, bringing Julie back to the apartment. Julie looked at her friend.

"I'm thinking I really need a job and my own apartment, and that I really want to foster or adopt."

33

Anthony walked beside Gideon, occasionally glancing at his cousin and Ryan on his other side. Williamsburg was bustling around them, moms pushing infants in strollers, joggers weaving through the streets. He had been on his way to Gideon's apartment, only to run into him and Ryan at the corner deli.

They'd been on their way for a walk and invited Anthony along. He couldn't help feel he was third-wheeling on a private conversation, but he needed to talk to Gideon. Which made Ryan the third-wheel.

Gideon scratched his jaw, lingering on the scruff he'd started keeping. Anthony had filled Ryan in on the situation with his mom and dad — briefly, he didn't think Ryan needed to hear his more insecure thoughts — and Gideon had taken on a concerned look. Ryan walked beside them, hands in his pockets.

"I mean, you need to talk to your dad, Ant."

Anthony rolled his eyes. "Yeah, I know that. I just literally haven't seen him. And he doesn't want to know anything about her."

"I hate to ask, but could you play the 'you're a parent and this is my life' card?" Ryan tilted his head, blonde crew cut reflecting the mid-afternoon sun.

"How do you mean?"

"Well, he's your parent," Ryan began. "He should know what's happening in your life, and how you're feeling. Especially when it comes to your mom. Could you just tell him you need to talk, and then tell him you need to talk to him about it and that he needs to listen since... he's your parent?"

Gideon glanced at Anthony. They'd both had complicated familial relationships; they were both only children, and while Anthony's mom had taken off when they were eighteen, Gideon's father had passed away when they were fifteen and Tom, his brother, had taken care of Gideon and his mom as much as he could. But Ryan had grown up in a 'normal' household — parents who loved one another and showered the excess on their three children.

"Is that what you do?" Anthony asked.

"Set boundaries and talk about emotions with my family? Yeah, it is." There was no judgement in Ryan's response, just a simple statement of facts.

Anthony thought about it. He and his dad had never really spoken about his mom, more so because his dad had a habit of sidestepping the topic or flat out saying he didn't want to discuss it. The divorce had been physically easier than most — his parents never went to court and, as far as Anthony knew, never even saw each other after she'd disappeared. But that left plenty of room for emotional toil, and time created space for those feelings to build without release.

They reached McCarren Park and Gideon led them through the winding paths in silence. While Gideon and Anthony had grown up together, Ryan and Lucas had joined them as a pair of best friends. The four of them had spent their formative college years writing music and partying, but moving into adulthood had kept their friendships right where they'd started. It was refreshing knowing he could lean on Ryan if he wanted or needed to.

Anthony broke the silence. "I guess I could try it. Thanks, man. I appreciate it."

"Sure thing. I dunno, my family was always really open about that stuff. I think it's healthier, in general. To be honest with each another."

"How are things with Julie?" Gideon asked.

The reminder made Anthony's head swim with all the conversations he needed to have. He'd never had this many serious conversations when he was intoxicated. "Fine. We had a nice phone call the other night and we're going to meet sometime this week. Actually, I've been meaning to ask if we could use your apartment to talk."

Ryan and Gideon stopped in their tracks, their faces amplifying how absurd the request sounded. Anthony had felt it as soon as the words slipped out.

"Dude... No." Gideon shook his head and kept walking. "You can be an adult and just have a conversation with her. Go to a park or something. Jesus, it's like you're fifteen."

Ryan laughed heartily, the sound scaring away a pack of pigeons hunting for seeds.

"Just thought I'd ask." Anthony shrugged, embarrassment creeping into his cheeks.

"Yeah, well, apparently she asked Ella and was

told the same thing." Gideon grumbled something else under his breath.

"What was that?"

"I said, you guys are like two peas in a pod. Can't wait to hear what she thinks of you and Ruby."

It was Anthony's turn to stop walking. He watched their backs recede, waiting for his cousin to face him. But Gideon kept his head down and moved forward.

"Dude. That was a low blow."

Gideon stopped, throwing his head back while Ryan looked between the two of them. Anthony thought he heard Gideon sigh as he turned around.

"How do you figure? You slept with her coworker. Then you dated her coworker. I can't wait to hear what Julie thinks, because you *know* she'll have words for you."

"I — "

"You need to at least take responsibility for that. Julie broke up with you seven months ago. Okay, so what? It happens. She's back. You can't hold it against her forever, not if you want to be with her. And you can't be pissed or upset with however she feels about you and Ruby." Gideon shrugged and kept walking, leaving Ryan to wait in the space between them.

Anthony started walking, passing Ryan to catch up to Gideon. His cousin was right, even if Anthony couldn't admit it aloud. He and Ryan walked beside Gideon in silence, reaching the end of the park.

"So, who's hungry?" Gideon asked.

34

The coffee shop down the street from the Maven Media office was packed with a lunchtime rush. Julie looked around, remembering how she came to this same spot last summer to meet Anthony for the first time in over a year. She'd been tasked by Ella, Gideon, and Tom with keeping an eye on him and his sobriety while they were on tour with Eternal Youths.

Sitting in the back corner facing the barista counter and large windows overlooking the Dumbo street, Julie sat at the same table Anthony had chosen all those months ago. Wood bench seating on one side, a metal chair on the other. Julie had grabbed a second chair in case Ella or Rachel didn't want to squeeze beside her on the bench. They had updates for her on the nonprofit launch, and she'd pushed for them to meet in a coffee shop.

She wasn't ready to face Ruby.

Julie heard Ella before she saw her, the big belly laugh announcing her entrance to the shop. Rachel followed, her more reserved chuckle barely heard above the din. She waved them over, skipping their usual hug given the tight space. Ella sat in the extra metal chair beside Julie while Rachel took the chair opposite, her dark hair further deepened from being backlit.

"Thanks so much for meeting me." Julie tried to contain her excitement but couldn't stop smiling.

"Of course!" Rachel pulled some paper from her black leather tote bag.

Ella cleared her throat. "But Jules? Eventually, we will have to meet at the office."

"I know, I know." Julie averted her gaze from Ella, focusing on the papers in front of Rachel. "So... What's the sitch?"

"Okay," Rachel started, clearing her throat and passing out her papers. "Long story short, since you've been gone, we've hired Tratz and Leibman Law as the company's lawyers. We spoke to them about this, and basically what they need from us is to figure out a name, figure out what our corporate structure is, and then recruit people for the various office positions, such as a minimum of one person for Incorporator and three for Director. There's a lot of filing and license obtaining; Tratz and Leibman will act as our Registered Agent for legal paperwork. The majority of what we can do right now is lay the ground work: figure out who we are and find people to help run it. We can't do any fundraising or solicitation until we obtain 501(c) status and apply for tax exemptions."

Julie flipped through the papers she'd been handed, scanning the more in-depth descriptions of each step.

"Wow."

"Yeah. It's a lot." Rachel sighed. "We also spoke to our accountant. We have room in the budget for a few new employees. Business is steadying, so we'd originally planned on hiring new staff to offload some of the work from the current employees. But we actually think it'd make sense to invest some of that money in this, since it's a way for the company to continue growing while business is slower."

"We think you would be a perfect fit as the Chief Executive," Ella chimed in. "We don't have the funds to pay you as a proper CEO, but it would be slightly higher than what you were receiving when you did our contracts. Since this is just starting and you'd be in charge of building the nonprofit from the ground up, you'd be tasked with developing and recruiting the initial directors, hiring staff, creating a fundraising plan, building a strategic framework for the business, and overseeing that tasks are done efficiently and effectively. How does that sound?"

"Like a dream. When can I start?" Julie felt warmth spread through her body. Working with her best friends again and as the CEO of a nonprofit that was her idea? An organization to help empower, and educate at-risk women and children?

She'd built her life around the idea of being a lawyer. Julie thought she'd be happy once she finished school. She thought she'd be happy once she got a job. She thought she'd be happy if she stuck with that job. If someone had told her — even a year ago — that she'd find a new dream, a real dream, and that it would be realized at the expense of being a lawyer, she wouldn't have believed them.

She couldn't have imagined being so happy.

"Next week. Welcome back, Julie." Rachel held her hand out, and they shook on it.

35

The apartment seemed so much smaller now that it was filled with the members of Eternal Youths. Tom preferred having them here for conversations instead of renting a practice room or doing things over the computer or phone. But Tom had stepped out; he still hadn't spoken more than two words to Anthony, and nothing outside of band business. Anthony looked around at his bandmates, broad shoulder to broad shoulder, long legs cramped to make room for the coffee table. They laughed without a care in the world, just happy to be there.

"Okay, guys." Tom's voice could be heard down the entry hallway, the sound of the door shutting and the bags rustling. He was an elephant on the hardwood as he walked into the kitchen, setting the bags on the island and looking at the crew. "I got some more snacks and a few drinks. Grab some, I have some good news."

The guys jumped up and rushed the island. Anthony followed behind Gideon, watching as everyone emptied the bags. Ginger beer, three different sodas... a bottle of whiskey and a couple six packs of beer. Gideon stopped short, causing Anthony to bump into him. He tried to catch his dad's eye, but Tom was busy fixing himself a whiskey and Coke. Lucas and Ryan grabbed beers. Max joined Gideon and Anthony.

The Sober Triangle.

They exchanged looks before easing towards the island. The others had emptied back to the living room, leaving them to face the vice they'd forfeited and the less-than-satisfying replacements. Anthony watched Gideon eye the whiskey but grab a Coke instead. Max grabbed a bottle of seltzer, and Anthony grabbed a ginger beer.

But not before glancing at the whiskey.

It had always been his and Gideon's downfall. He couldn't figure out why his dad would go out of his way to put alcohol in front of his sober son and nephew.

Anthony didn't have time to find an answer before Tom called them back into the living room.

"Time for a toast — Nate called me yesterday and said the engineers had finished mastering the new album! They're choosing July 31st for release."

The guys raised their glasses, whooping and hollering.

"Secondly, since we'll be touring with Imagine Dragons from August through November, Nate figures we can festival tour again and release singles and pre-order codes for May through July. Then hit the ground running when we start the fall tour. So prepare yourselves for touring May through November!"

They all stood, clinking their cans and glasses, side-hugging whoever was closest. Anthony smiled, briefly distracted from his dad purposefully bringing alcohol into the house. He had missed the festival tour last year; physical therapy and addiction recovery didn't mesh with the life of a traveling rock star. The rest of the band had gotten closer, and Anthony had had to make peace with that.

But when Anthony saw the way Gideon kept fidgeting with his hair and eyeing the tumbler in Tom's hand, he saw red. Gideon had slipped up once, three years ago. Just last year, he'd confided in Anthony just how much he missed drinking: the burn, the haze, the escape from reality. The fact his own dad would risk Gideon slipping because Anthony had reached out to his mom was almost too much to bear. He pushed his way through the guys to Tom. They were the same height, nose to nose, but Anthony had the element of surprise: he'd never confronted his dad before.

"What the fuck?" Anthony gritted his teeth, the words slicing through in a near-whisper.

Tom took a step back, almost falling back onto the couch, his drink dangerously climbing the sides of his glass. Anthony wished it fucking shattered.

"How could you bring alcohol here? Why?" His hushed words were loud in the ensuing silence.

His dad just stared at him. His gray eyes became steel, his spine a metal rod. Tom crossed his arms and stepped forward.

"Because I wanted a drink, Anthony. This is my house, my apartment. If you don't like it, feel free to move."

Anthony wanted to clean out his ears.

"What happened to the band deciding a few years ago to be sober? Three of the members are alcoholics and you're just going to bring alcohol to band meetings without so much as a warning?"

"You're right, we should've voted on it. I figured Gideon's been sober for over two years, and you've almost hit the year mark. I'm sorry, Max, I should've asked how you felt." Tom pursed his lips. "But right now, we're in my house."

"Is this about mom?" Anthony couldn't stop the words from slipping out. They'd been at the forefront of his mind since the whiskey bottle was revealed.

Tom shifted his gaze to the room behind Anthony. "You guys heading out?"

Anthony turned, everyone standing awkwardly with their jackets.

"Um... Yeah, Tom," Max said, shrugging his shoulders. "You guys have things to figure out."

The guys darted before Tom had a chance to push past Anthony. With the final click of the door, he turned to face his son. His face was more lined than usual, mouth downturned in disappointment.

"I don't have anything to figure out, Anthony. This is my house. If you have any issues with how I run things, you can leave."

36

Julie closed the laptop, her brain burning with all the information she'd read. Padding from her bedroom to the kitchen, she put the kettle on for tea before leaning against the counter, cool, even through her pajama top.

She probably wouldn't have granite counters in her new apartment.

After her meeting with Ella and Rachel, she'd immediately gone home to look up apartments and had spent all weekend sorting how she wanted her future to look. Julie would be forever be grateful to Rachel's father for allowing her to live in his apartment rent free, but it was past time to find her own place, and with the salary she'd be getting as CEO of her nonprofit, she could find a nice two or three bedroom a little closer to work. She'd love to stay in Manhattan, but at this point, she didn't care where she lived.

Even if it was Brooklyn.

At this point, she'd decided she was ready to move forward with what she loved more than anything else: helping children.

Julie was waiting for Rachel and Ella to come home so she could get their thoughts on Julie applying to become a foster parent in the next couple of years. It was Monday — when Ella had lived with them, they spent Mondays live-tweeting their comments on various movies from the company account. Even though Ella had moved out, she still made a point to come over on Mondays to join in the laughter and boxed wine.

As if on cue, the front door opened and Julie heard them kick off their shoes. They were laughing as they entered the kitchen from the long hall. Julie loved when Ella came over; Rachel was visibly more happy.

"Hey, Jules!" Ella gave her a big hug. "Tea on a Monday? No boxed wine?"

"Oh, definitely! Just later. Let me know what takeout you guys want and I'll order. Do you know when Ben will be home?" Julie passed them a stack of menus before pouring her tea. It'd be nice if he could be there, but she didn't want him walking into the room when they were in the middle of a conversation he had no information about.

"No idea, you know how publishing is. He'll probably be home around nine," Rachel said. "I'm going to go change into pajamas, but I think we should just get a couple of pizzas and some wings. Make it easy." She tossed the menus back on the island before disappearing down the hall. Ella agreed and took after her.

Julie placed the order, finishing as the other two came back. Rachel had donned one of her silky pajama sets, a French blue that shone silver against her sepia skin. Ella had thrown on an old pair of gray sweats with a large, faded floral print and an old T-shirt, the pink highlighting her rosy cheeks. They looked cozy, happy, relaxed, and Julie felt bad for ruining it.

"Food will be here in an hour. I — I want to ask you guys something." Julie held her hot mug in both hands, letting the burn sit on her palms as a distraction from the anxiety, the magnitude, of what she needed to say.

"Anything, babe." Ella leaned against the island.

"So a few things," Julie blew on her tea, working

up the courage. "After our meeting, I got to thinking I should find my own place and start building what I want my life to look like in five years. Between volunteering in India and now the nonprofit, I've realized my calling is to help kids. And when I thought more about how much I missed my kids in India, and I how I couldn't wait to help the mothers and children here, I realized something else." She took a deep breath and looked at each of her friends. They only stared back, giving her the space she needed to keep going.

"I realized that I want kids. My own, one day, for sure. But in the meantime, I want to foster. I feel like I lost all this time trying to build a life that would make my parents happy. Traveling alone for six months showed me I wasn't waiting on anyone but myself. And I'm tired of waiting."

Ella just smiled, having been let in on secret. But Rachel stared at her, mouth agape, hanging in the silence that followed until she burst into a smile and almost into tears, rushing to give Julie a hug. Julie was barely able to set her tea down before the force pushed her into the counter, and she laughed while the normally composed Rachel blubbered into her hair.

"Why are you so upset? It's okay! I promise." She

hugged her friend, feeling Rachel's arms squeeze her waist. "I know I'm single and in my late twenties, but I looked into the application and I meet the requirements. Especially, say, a year from now when the nonprofit's set up and I live in my own two or three bedroom. I've just... I've never felt so sure about something."

Julie met Ella's eyes over the top of Rachel's bowed head. "I think that's a really lovely idea, Julie. Obviously, there's a lot to it, but if anyone would be a good fit, it'd be you." Ella joined their little huddle.

When Rachel pulled away, wiping her face with her long sleeves, her eyes were almost puffed closed. Julie smoothed the plastered hair from her forehead.

"What's wrong?"

"I just — I didn't know you wanted to be a mom but you'd be so great. A—And I'm just — I'm just so happy for you. Sorry, I just wasn't expecting this." She sobered and placed her hands on Julie's shoulders. "Is this for Hannah?"

Julie tried to take a step back, the words catching her off guard. Was it for Hannah? She hadn't thought they'd be directly linked but... she'd always felt guilty Hannah had been robbed of the rest of her life. And she'd felt so heartbroken at the children in India who'd been robbed of parents. Maybe the need to help started with Hannah, and ended with fostering being the only thing she felt capable of doing.

"I — I actually don't know, Rachel. Maybe. Probably."

"Well, whatever the reason, I'm happy for you. Please let me know what I can do to help." Rachel rubbed her hand along Julie's back. "In the meantime, shall we pick a movie?"

"Yes." Julie smiled. She hadn't expected the conversation to go the way it had, and she couldn't wait to get started.

37

Anthony exited the subway, getting turned around as he tried to make his way out of Grand Central.

It didn't help he was nervous as fuck.

He navigated the streets to reach the Mediterranean restaurant on East 45th and Vanderbilt, scanning the crowds for a tall, black-haired woman with eyes the color of indigo. Bouncing on the balls of his feet while he waited out front, his heart skipped a beat at every ebony head until they turned and he saw they weren't Christine Russo.

Christine Scott.

"Anthony?"

He froze, the voice coming from behind him; he'd been looking in the wrong direction.

Inching to face the woman whose voice was

softer than he'd remembered, Anthony tried to steel himself against what he saw. Bottomless pools of blue surrounded by deep crow's feet — she smiled often, except now, when her lips remained parted in a state of disbelief.

"It's really you." It came as a whisper, and she looked him up and down. They were almost the same height, her dark hair streaked with pearl. She reached an arm out as if to hug him but hesitated and started to pull back. Anthony watched the motion, the moment almost disappearing before he realized he needed to act. He pulled her into his warmth, feeling the substantial fold of her body into his. The gravity of a love he'd been missing, centering them.

Anthony wasn't sure how much time passed before they separated. He had to resist the urge to stare at this woman who bore him, who he bore a resemblance to, but they were perfect strangers.

"Shall we go in?" Christine shoved her hands in her pockets, glancing down the street.

"Oh, um, yeah. Sure. After you," Anthony said, pulling the door open for her to step through.

The restaurant was colossal and bright. Peach drapes hung from the soaring windows that made up one wall, matching the accent umbrellas and lamps hanging from the ceiling. Columns, masoned with jagged grey-white stone, interspersed between the many tables littering the great room.

"Hello, how can we help you?" The bright-eyed hostess looked at him, hair sleeked back into a high ponytail.

"Oh um, we have a reservation. Under Scott." Anthony cleared his throat, feeling out of place. When his mom had suggested the place close to where her train got in, he hadn't thought to look it up. He'd never been to a high-end Mediterranean restaurant and didn't think this would be any different. He looked down at his worn jeans, his shoes just short of needing duct tape.

He wouldn't make that mistake again.

The hostess gathered two menus and led them to a table against the back stone wall, a substantial but simple gold-framed mirror hanging in the middle. Christine slid into the booth while Anthony took the chair opposite, thanking the hostess. By the time she disappeared and he'd settled in, Christine — his mom — was already looking through the menu.

"I think we should get a bottle of the cabernet blend to start." She didn't look up from the menu.

Anthony couldn't help but just stare. The woman

before him was nothing like the vibrant woman he remembered from his youth. She was... disinterested. Anthony felt the consequence of going against what his father had said. He felt like he was back in that awful morning, seeing the empty slivers on the bookshelves.

Disinterested. Gone.

"Anthony?" Christine looked up, eyes clear of any of the emotion he'd glimpsed when they first met.

"Sorry." He cleared his throat. 'Um, you can get a glass. I'm sober."

"Oh. Well, where's the fun in that?" She laughed but shook her head in disbelief. Anthony felt himself shrink into his chair.

The waitress came over and took Christine's drink order. Anthony ordered a Coke.

"So... Why did you reach out to me, Anthony?"

Anthony furrowed his brow. "You mean aside from the fact that you left when I was eighteen and ignored every message I left you? And you agreed that we should talk, so it sounded like you have something to say to me?"

And you called me honey.

He pushed the thought from his brain but not before it rolled through him like thunder, tearing into every wall he'd built to protect the boy she'd left behind.

Christine sighed and tapped her fingers against the table, muffled by the thick linen tablecloth.

"We do need to talk. And you're right to be angry. And I'm sorry."

"Yeah, all of that is nice but I need to know why. I don't care what the reason is, I just need to hear you say it."

She lowered her head, mumbling. "I just... I couldn't do it. I know, it's not an excuse. I just woke up one morning and had this... intense hatred for my life. I was doing the same thing, day in and day out. You know, no one ever tells you the hardest thing about life is the monotony. It was the same thing every day. And then your dad stopped asking me about my day, you kept pushing back, and I was stuck trying to keep everything running and hold myself together." She glanced at him before returning her focus to the silverware in front of her. "I know this is hard to hear, and unfair. But you deserve the truth. I dreamt of escaping. For years. After your uncle passed, your dad spent so much time with Amelia and Gideon. I felt even more isolated, even more forgotten. And you were out, getting into trouble and being a disobedient teen.

You guys didn't need me, and I didn't have anything left to give you guys. Once you turned eighteen, I couldn't bear the thought of another hour in that godforsaken house. And I was past the point of done; I needed a new life."

Her story was everything Anthony had feared, but it was still a relief to hear her say it out loud. Now the voice in his head had an echo, and he could stop feeling crazy for thinking his mom didn't love him.

"So you found another house to disappear into? Another man to stop seeing you, and two new kids to disappoint you?"

Christine shrugged. "Life is weird and funny and you never know why things happen the way they do, Anthony. I moved back home to Connecticut, took up in my hometown. And one day I was in the grocery store and ran into my high school sweetheart. He was also divorced and had sole custody of his two girls. Somehow that house didn't feel like a prison. They listened to me. They needed me. And after the divorce was final and you stopped messaging me, it was easier to forget than to fix something that would never be whole."

Anthony held his head in his hands, trying to sort through everything she'd said while feeling an immense rage rise through him. He'd known what she was going to say, and while it was a relief to hear her admit it, he couldn't shake the feeling that she was just... mean. Not a good mother. And that there was nothing he could do to have the mother he so desperately wanted, the mother he thought he'd had. He took several deep breaths.

"Okay. I can't do this right now."

Anthony stood and walked out, leaving her in the fancy restaurant with her mouth hanging open. He didn't look back.

38

The apartment phone connected to the building's front desk rang, and Julie peered down the hall. It rang again, and she set the leftover container on the island to answer it. It was after ten; there was no possible reason they should be calling her.

When she picked up the phone the man at the front desk claimed there was a guest for Julie Milligan.

"I'm sorry, who's the guest?"

She heard a muffled exchange. "He says his name is Anthony Russo."

"I'm sorry?" *What the fuck?*

"Anthony Russo."

She looked at the phone, her face twisted in confusion. This had to be some sort of prank.

But it was still Anthony, and she wanted to see him.

"Send him up. Thank you, have a good rest of your night." Julie hung up the phone and looked down at her pajamas. Yoga pants, an old shirt, and some cat socks. Nowhere near as nice as Rachel's pajamas, but certainly more refined than Ella's. She wiped her face for any stray makeup smudges or food smears and tousled her hair, hoping it had a bedhead effect.

The knock on her door made her start, and she had to resist the urge to immediately open the door. Julie stopped herself just in time; he didn't need to know she was waiting for him.

When she did open the door, his hand was poised to knock again.

"Hey. Sorry for coming so late." Anthony lowered his hand, pulling his jacket tighter around him. "I can leave if you're in the middle of something."

"No, no, it's okay. Come in." Julie stepped inside, the proximity to his body dizzying. She felt his cool eyes searching her face to make sure it was actually okay that he arrived on her doorstep late on a work night. While she felt herself blush, she could hope he would read it for what it was: he could show up on her doorstep anytime, and she would always open the door.

She didn't look at him as he entered the apartment, his spicy scent enough to send her down the hall faster than normal. Julie reached the kitchen and heard him take off his shoes and jacket, padding in her footsteps. When he entered the room, she was pressed against the edge of the sink to give as much space between then as she could.

If Julie thought being close to him was dizzying, she hadn't accounted for seeing him — jacket-less — in her kitchen. The man she knew every inch of wore a henley, covering the scars he'd sustained from his car accident. But it stretched along his shoulders, molded along the defined peaks and valleys of his torso. His jeans were stretched along his hips, tight against his thighs. Somehow she forced herself to look at his face.

The kitchen lights were starry reflections in the navy galaxy of his eyes. They were bright, almost wet, as if he'd been upset.

The last time she'd seen that was the morning she'd broken his heart.

"Anthony... What's wrong?" Julie ignored her brain screaming to stay put, instead following the call of her body to his. Placing a tentative hand on the bulge of his bicep, she tried to ignore the corded muscle as she led him to the living room, guiding him to sit on the couch. She sat on the opposite side, not wanting to crowd him.

He sat down with a heavy sigh, wrapping his arms around himself as he leaned back, legs outstretched.

"I saw my mom tonight."

Julie took a deep breath and held it, trying to imagine what had been said to send him here.

Back to her.

39

Anthony hadn't known where else to go.

He had felt his feet carry him away from the restaurant, away from a woman who carried the title of mother but no other aspect of the word. Had felt his legs bring him through subways and over broken concrete sidewalks to the front door of a luxury apartment building. A stranger's voice gave Julie's name to the front desk clerk.

It hadn't clicked that he'd gone to her apartment until the door swung open and he saw her standing there.

Looking over at her now, he felt like he'd been hit by a truck. She had let him into her apartment as if nothing had happened between them. She sat there, her legs curled under her, watching him. Hearing him recount what had happened in the restaurant. Listening to what was between the words, how nothing could have prepared him for being treated so openly unwanted by his own mom.

They sat there in silence after he spoke. Anthony watched her chew the inside of her mouth, staring at the coffee table. When Julie returned his stare, Anthony saw her flushed skin and the hard set of her mouth tempered by wet eyes.

"I'm so sorry, Anthony."

He looked away and shrugged. "It's okay."

"But it's not." Her voice was firm, and she softened. "It's not, Anthony. That was mean and it hurt and it's not fair. I'm sorry you have to carry that. Will you see her again?"

He forced a laugh. "No. There's nothing left to say."

"Okay. So how will you move forward?"

"In what sense?"

"Now that you've reconnected with your mom and had this shitty conversation, what will you do to make sure you don't hold onto this — this anger and abandonment?"

Anthony cocked his head and looked at her,

really looked at her. Her earnest face, open, willing. The slope of her shoulders. She readjusted, now sitting cross-legged, her hands just sitting in her lap.

"You went to India and now you're a little guru, eh?" He tried to crack a smile, feeling it fall flat as soon as his mouth lifted.

But Julie picked it up, her petal lips parting to show the smile that lit his heart. "I mean, that's how it works right? Has absolutely nothing to do with my own mom basically disowning me."

"Right, right, right. Of course not. How is that going?" Anthony turned to face her, his long legs forcing him into a pretzel.

Julie shrugged and starting picking at a loose thread on the couch. "It's not. I need to talk to them but... I haven't really felt ready, you know? We haven't spoken since my mom blamed me for Hannah's death. I don't know what to say."

"So how are you making sure you're not holding onto any anger and abandonment?" He smiled at her, throwing her words back at her gently, wanting to hold her in his arms while she answered.

"Nice." She rolled her eyes. "I'm personally working on accepting that there's nothing I can do about how my mom sees me. I tried that, and it didn't work. Clearly — I felt the need to go off for six months, around the world, because who I was was not who I wanted to be. If I can see that she's a grieving mother with misplaced guilt and anger, and accept that she's doing her best while I'm doing my best, then I think that's enough for me to move forward peacefully."

"Easier said than done."

"Obviously, that's why I haven't spoken to her." Julie gave him a sad smile. "Thank you. For coming here."

"Thank you for opening the door. I'm sorry it's late. Where are the other two?" Anthony felt the dread creeping in at the idea of seeing her two roommates, both of whom hadn't shown much support in the past.

"Out still, but they'll probably be home soon. Why, you worried?" She stretched out her foot, tapping his leg with it. The touch sent a jolt through him. He resisted cupping her foot with his hand and rubbing his thumb along the ridge of her sole.

"I don't think I have anything to be worried about. I mean… You ended things with me, Julie."

She released a long, slow breath, averting her gaze to where her toes barely grazed his shin. "Yeah, I did. Do you want to talk about that right now?"

His hand reached for her the way he'd imagined, feeling her smooth skin against his palm.

"No, I don't. I want to enjoy this a little longer."

40

His hand was a shock against her skin, a memory she'd held onto for the last seven months.

Julie swallowed the lump in her throat, trying not to read into what he'd said.

I want to enjoy this a little longer.

As in, once we say what we need to say, this stolen moment of bliss won't exist anymore.

As in, I need a friend in you but nothing more.

She pressed her foot against his hand, wanting him to know that it was okay for him to touch her longer. That he could move his large, calloused hands up her shins, along her thighs, trailing the lengths of her arms to cup her face. That he could bring his face closer and start to close the distance she'd forced upon them.

Anthony squeezed her foot, his thumb running along the arch before letting go. He raised his eyes to hers, searching. For what, she didn't know. Julie would offer him anything he wanted to give them another chance. To give her another chance.

"I should head home," he said, "but let's do this again. Soon. I guess we're okay in haunted spaces after all." He rose, holding a hand out to help her up from the couch.

"I guess so." Julie laughed, taking the proffered palm. She stumbled and clutched his arm to keep steady, her body pressing against his. He was an assault on her senses, coiled muscles and ginger she wanted to lick from his skin. Her breath caught, and she tilted her head to his. His eyes were hooded as he took her in, tongue darting to lick his lips. Julie lifted a hand to his neck, her thumb tracing his jaw. She could almost taste paradise...

He pulled away and ran his hand through his hair, turning towards the door.

"Thank you, Julie."

She trailed him to the door. "Thanks for coming. Let me know what your schedule looks like this week, maybe Wednesday?

"Sure." He paused, turning around in the frame as if to say something but shook his head instead.

"I'll talk to you soon."

She watched him enter the elevator, hoping he'd turn around and say whatever it was he kept to himself. When he didn't look back, Julie closed the door behind her and went back to the kitchen, letting her mind drift to the polarizing options: *I love you, I miss you, let's try again. I hate you, this hurt too much, we shouldn't see each other.*

Julie sighed when she saw the pot abandoned on the stove, the leftover containers still empty on the island. She'd forgotten to put away her dinner. Stirring the cold soup to get rid of the film that had formed on top, she let herself get lost in the swirl of rice and corn, cilantro and chicken, the scent of chili powder and lime filling her nose.

He'd come to her because he needed a friend. One of the two people in life that was supposed to be there for him — love him — unconditionally had turned their back on him with a half-assed apology stamped across her shoulders. He didn't deserve that.

No one deserved that.

She felt the anger toward her own mother rise like a storm through her body. Slamming the emptied pot into the sink, the metal chipping a porcelain plate. Julie took a deep breath. She couldn't continue with her life if she held onto the past. Part of what was holding her back, she could tell herself, was her mother's blame for the accident ten years ago. Julie had worked through the guilt herself, but she hadn't worked through her mother's.

It wasn't her job to. She knew that. But she wondered if every child carried their parent's burdens as their own, waiting for the day when they'd wake up and magically be twenty years lighter. Julie wondered if that day would ever come for her. If she'd wake up one morning with a voicemail from her mom, apologizing and saying she loved her daughter.

Or if Julie needed to be the one to find the magic in accepting her mom was flawed, like everyone, and didn't deserve less love because of it.

41

The East Village streets were empty, even given the late hour. Anthony had taken the subway from Julie's place on the Upper West Side down to the West Village and walked the rest of the way to his apartment, enjoying the brisk air.

Julie's understanding of his situation was partly why he'd sought asylum at her place. Her own situation was another part. But seeing her had been the main reason. He needed to see if the way Julie had looked at him outside of the corner deli was a one-time fluke or if she meant what he saw.

It wasn't a fluke.

Anthony thought of her small hand, gentle, wrapped around his arm while she led him to the couch. The way her pajama pants had hugged curves he missed filling his hands. How she listened to him and then advised him, from her own struggles with her mom.

Accept and move on.

Anthony reached his apartment and looked up. The lights weren't on, but there was no saying if it was because Tom was asleep or wasn't home. Anthony paced the street. He didn't know what his dad was up to anymore. The confrontation at the band meeting had resulted in them avoiding each other at all costs; if Tom was sitting on the couch and Anthony entered the room, Tom would leave. They stopped cooking dinner together. And they didn't have the excuse of band meetings anymore — recording was over, and they wouldn't need to start rehearsals for tour for another month.

Not that that would magically heal whatever this rift was.

His dad had never acted like this. Even when Gideon — sober — had taken a sip from a flask Anthony pushed on him three years ago. Tom was the reasonable one to Anthony's carelessness. He was the steady one to Anthony's need for escape. He was stern, but not mean. If Anthony could just get him to stay in the room and talk.

Accept and move on.

Anthony climbed the stairs to the shared apartment, knowing he would have to move out soon. Not before they'd healed their relationship, but not long after. He opened the door, trying to tiptoe while knowing his weight made the move ineffective. The floors groaned with every step. When he made it to the kitchen, a shock white rectangle of paper glowed on the counter in the moonlight streaming through the window.

Anthony -

I've gone to the house in Sugar Grove. I needed some space. I'm sorry things have been so tense. We'll talk when I get back next month.

Love always,

Dad

He couldn't remember the last time his dad had left a note. Anthony couldn't say he was surprised at his dad leaving, but he also couldn't help but feel he'd missed a chance to repair things. Sure, they'd talk in a month. But what if too much time had passed? What if his dad decided his ex-wife was right, and some things weren't worth the uphill battle?

Anthony crumpled the note and tossed it in the trash can.

Halfway to his room, he stopped. He was alone

in the apartment. And he would be alone for the foreseeable future. He felt the pull of a lifetime of lonely midnights and returned to the kitchen, wondering if his dad had left the vices he'd so carelessly brought into the house.

Swinging open cupboard after cupboard, Anthony dug around. Nothing hidden in the large roasting pan kept in the cupboard above the stove. Nothing hidden by the cleaning supplies beneath the sink. Nothing in the back of the junk drawer, hidden behind old address labels and mismatched card decks. Anthony surveyed the room, out of options. Now it wasn't so much a matter of drinking what he missed so much; he just wanted to know if his dad had left alcohol in the house with his alcoholic son.

Anthony went to his dad's bedroom, momentarily stopped by the effect of a closed door to a room he didn't belong in. But his dad wasn't there, and Anthony was more curious about what was kept in the room. He opened the door, observing before entering. He'd never been in here before; his dad always kept the door closed, and there was never any reason for Anthony to go in.

It looked like any other boring bedroom: queen-size bed across from the closet, two nightstands on either side, a dresser under the double windows. No art, no books, no music. Anthony dropped to the hardwood floor to peek under the bed.

Empty.

He checked the dresser drawers; how many socks could one person own?

Nothing outside of clothes.

That left the closet.

Anthony slid open the doors, seeing the shelf above the rods. It was covered with random shit. He thanked his height for being able to partially see while his hand felt around clothes and bags and —

A box.

A cliched movie move, Anthony still couldn't suppress his curiosity. He set the old photo box down on the bed before going back to finish his closet inspection. The side he started on proved useless — other than the box — so he slid the doors to check the other side.

Clothes, clothes, jackpot.

He pulled down the whiskey Tom had bought for the band meeting. He held the smooth glass in his hand, the amber liquid sloshing inside the half-empty bottle. Wondering how far was too far. Had he crossed the line, hunting for the bottle? Holding it? Would he be able to turn back if he uncapped it, smelled the burning oak and wished it set fire to his throat?

Gripping the cap in his hand, he wiggled until the cork popped free. A cloud of spicy orange rose from the bottle, filling the small room.

He wanted to gag.

He wanted to meet oblivion.

He wanted to be the man he promised himself he was.

Anthony took the bottle into the kitchen, watching the elixir bubble before it fell down the drain. He ran hot water into the empty bottle, letting the memories of drunken nights and stupid decisions burn away until the scent disappeared.

A wave of exhaustion rolled through him. He'd proven he could step back if he needed — wanted — to. He threw the bottle in the trash, not wanting another reminder of the person he'd been. He just wanted to go to bed.

42

Julie paced her room, the upcoming week looming over her. She was starting back at Maven Media in a few days. She didn't even know if her professional clothes still fit, she'd have to get used to having a work schedule again, she'd have to see Ruby…

She wanted to throw up.

What she really wanted to do was talk with Anthony, find out what page they were on.

He'd shown Julie vulnerability, when he'd come to her door. It was a side of him she'd had to pry to see last summer, when he was guarded and deflected every question she'd thrown at him. Not that she'd been any better.

But time was a funny thing, and she was not the same person. Based on what she saw, he wasn't either. He'd run from the meeting with his mom, knowing what his limits were. Julie had done that when she'd run from her mom last year. As much as she preached to him about accepting and moving on, she still had a long way to go with her own family. A long way that could be started if Julie would just pick up the phone and call.

She chewed on her thumbnail, stopping in front of the phone at the foot of her bed. It was a hectic week to begin with, an emotional one, but holding onto resentment and anger towards her mom wouldn't help. This was one of those times when she needed to be an adult.

Releasing a deep breath, she dialed her dad's number. Carty answered on the first ring, his gentle voice betraying excitement and confusion.

"Juliette! What a lovely surprise, I wasn't expecting you to call."

"Hi, dad. I'm sorry I didn't call sooner. I've — I've been busy." Julie crawled onto her bed, anticipating the need to be surrounded by fluffy pillows and soft blankets.

"I figured as much, especially with all the traveling. I — we — miss you."

Julie stopped herself from laughing, knowing there was no 'we' in that statement.

"Dad, you know we need to talk about last summer. With mom and Grandma and Grandpa."

He sighed. "I know, honey. I want to. But I don't know if your mom is ready to have that conversation yet."

"She was really mean," Julie whispered. "And she's had since the accident to have that conversation with me. It's been over ten years."

Carty was silent.

"Dad, if Mom won't talk to me, can you just tell me how you feel?"

Another sighed and the creak of footsteps. She could see him walking from where he'd answered the phone — probably the kitchen — to his favorite armchair in the family room. The soft plop of him sitting down, legs falling onto the ottoman.

"Juliette, I have never thought it was your fault, that accident. You were always too careful, too worried about anything happening to her. As soon as the police report came back stating the other driver ran a red thinking it'd already changed to green, my feelings were concrete." He sniffled, and Julie could see the tall proud man who was still trying to hide his emotions from her, even over the phone. "I have always and will always love you. I am proud of you. You've always lived your life to the fullest. You've always been strong. Not just for yourself, but for me and your mom. I'm sorry this was the hand we were dealt."

"Do you think she'll ever be ready to have that conversation?"

"I don't know, honey. I've tried to talk to her, but she shuts down. I think everyone deals with hurt in their own way, and for your mother, she prefers to deal with it alone. All we can do is love."

Julie wondered at her own path of moving forward, of acceptance. She knew love factored in there somewhere, and was a little surprised that that was her dad's chosen coping mechanism. Especially with someone like her mom, who had edges harder than most.

"How do you do that?" she asked.

"Love?"

Julie laughed at the seemingly simple question. "Yeah. How do you love when you haven't forgiven?"

"Well..." She heard the scratch of his fingers in his short beard. "Well, I think you just accept the person for who they are. We're all working through things the best we can. Your mother has made her fair share of mistakes. At the end of the day, even when I disagree — hell, especially when I disagree — I just try and remember that I love her, and the rest sorts itself out. Eventually the forgiveness comes, but it needs space. So we love."

Acceptance equaled love equaled forgiveness equaled acceptance.

Carty was on Step 2 of moving forward, whereas Julie was still on Step 1. But if her father — who had lost one daughter to fate, the other to running away, and his wife to grief — could do it, she certainly could.

"It takes time, honey," he added, as if reading her thoughts. "I've had a lifetime to work on it. What really helped me was deciding how I wanted to feel. I didn't want to feel hurt and angry all the time. I didn't want to despair. And when you give yourself the choice of love or despair, I think it becomes pretty clear."

Julie knew all about deciding how to feel; she'd done it with her career, her goals. She'd done it with Anthony. She could do it with her mom.

"I should probably call her, right?"

Carty chuckled. "At some point, yes. It's only as big a deal as you make it, but only you can determine how big a deal is worth it."

Julie nodded, even though he couldn't see. It made sense, and it showed where she needed to work on herself more.

If she was going to work in a field helping women and children — if she was serious about fostering — she needed to apply what she'd learned in India and what her dad was confirming.

Acceptance, love, forgiveness.

43

Anthony grabbed his coffee mug. He was still adjusting to having his dad gone, not running into the gray-haired giant in the hallway or playfully arguing over who would get to the coffee pot first. He'd crashed on Gideon's couch for a few nights following the whiskey incident. He needed space from himself, something the apartment offered none of.

But he was back, feeling stronger than when he'd left. He had one task today: open the box he'd found in his dad's closet. Anthony knew it'd been wrong of him to poke around, but there was a part of him that wondered what Tom was hiding from him. Maybe something to do with his mom and how she could be so cold to Anthony. Maybe something about his own past and why he'd shut Anthony out. Maybe something about his brother, Gideon's father.

Wandering down the hall, he stopped in front of his dad's door. It was ajar from the other night, when Anthony had dumped the bottle and grabbed an overnight bag to take to Gideon's. He pushed it open with a finger, ignoring the goosebumps and irrational fear of something jumping out from behind the bed.

Nope. No jumps. Just the dusty photo box sitting at the foot of the bed.

It looked like something found at a craft store for old ladies that liked to scrapbook. The print would be lovingly called *vintage* instead of the more apt *grandma floral*. The whites were yellowed; this box had seen some things. Anthony set his mug on one of the nightstands and sat cross-legged in the middle of the bed, steeling himself for whatever might be hidden away. Taking a deep breath, he lifted the lid. It stuck, and he lifted and shimmied until the box fell away from the lid, landing with a soft pop. The musty smell that escaped was one only associated with old letters.

Anthony peered into the box. An old bible, a leather cord, an envelope. A stack of letters.

Lifting up the bible, he cracked open its pages.

His father wasn't religious, that he knew of. Anthony had never gone to a church, and his parents had never spoken at length about religion; they'd always wanted him to find his own way. The pages held no markings. It was just old, and he set it aside. He pulled out the leather cord. It was a necklace with no pendant — just the little silver ring a pendant had once hung from. He set it on top of the bible, reaching for the envelope next.

Pictures. Old pictures, ones of a young Tom in arms with a slightly older boy. A couple of photos with both boys and their parents. A few of Anthony as a baby. One of Gideon's parents with a baby Gideon. One of Gideon's mom, Amelia.

Just Amelia.

Anthony's heart started pounding. Was it odd for his divorced dad to have a picture of his widowed sister-in-law — just her? He couldn't tell, but his mom's words came ringing back: *After your uncle passed, your dad spent so much time with Amelia and Gideon.*

He put the pictures back into the envelope and set it beside the other treasures. Staring at the stack of letters left in the box, Anthony let out a slow breath and delicately picked up the pile. He opened the letter on top, finding the date scrawled in the top right corner. October 2006.

A year and a half after Gideon's father passed.

Anthony's eyes darted from the Dearest Thomas to the Always, Amelia on the back of the page. He felt his blood pumping through his body, the room becoming unbearably hot and cold at the same time. He picked up the letter from the bottom of the pile.

February 2008. Dearest Thomas. Always, Amelia.

Four months before Christine left Tom.

The letter fell from his hands. His father had engaged in handwritten letters with Gideon's mom for a year and a half. It could be nothing. The brothers had always been close, them and their spouses often going out and spending time together. But too many pieces fit a story Anthony didn't want to be true.

The lone picture of Amelia, smiling at the camera like she loved the person behind it.

Letters spanning a year and a half.

After your uncle passed, your dad spent so much time with Amelia and Gideon.

Anthony knew he shouldn't read the letters. He shouldn't have found them in the first place. But knowing his dad had kept this from him — from

Gideon — all these years, knowing that this was the straw that broke the camel's back with his mom... Anthony thought he owed it to himself to know the truth.

Grabbing the stack and his coffee mug, he slammed the bedroom door behind him as he made his way to the living room. Anthony didn't know what he'd find hidden within the meticulous cursive. He just knew he needed the truth, and he needed it from someone other than his father.

44

Julie stopped in the communal bathroom in the office building to check herself before her first day in the office. The building bathrooms had the most flattering full-length mirrors, a perfect excuse for putting off having to walk into Maven Media and see Ruby Delacey. She knew neither of them owed the other anything. She would just rather not have to work beside her ex's ex — or current thing, she actually didn't know if they were still seeing each other — without speaking to her first.

Especially since she wanted to win him back.

She'd decided black pointed toe heels and a black sheath dress would be the most flattering against her fair skin and gold hair. Julie added a sheer *dupatta* as a drapey shawl; the traditional

Indian head scarf had been a gift from an elderly shopkeeper she visited regularly and whose sister hand embroidered them with glittery thread and seed beads. It was also black, but that only highlighted the aqua trim and silver embroidered flowers. Carrying a piece of India with her gave her a sense of peace for the lion's den.

Smoothing her dress and touching up her makeup, Julie gave herself a final pep talk.

This was what she wanted. This was what she'd sacrificed her old life — her old love — for.

It was now or never.

The click of her heels on the polished concrete echoed through the industrial building as she passed individual office spaces. She'd missed that sound; it always made her think of strong, intelligent women taking care of business. Stopping in front of Maven Media's bamboo door, she took a deep breath. Julie keyed in the code on the security pad and pushed open the door.

Maven Media was situated in the Brooklyn neighborhood of Dumbo along the East River. Located between the Manhattan and Brooklyn bridges, the periodic rattling of the subway cars had became the sound of home. Julie faced the back wall of windows, taking in the brightly lit space. The kitchen was still on the right. She remembered when she'd first started, just her, Rachel, and Ella. The office had been spacious. Since Julie left, someone had squeezed in a few more desks. The space was beginning to look cramped, and that was before the work day had even started.

Rachel looked up from her desk in front of the back wall, standing with a smile.

"Yay, you're back! Sorry I had you come in so early, I just wanted to go over a few things with you. Ella would've been here but she needed to meet with Eternal Youths' label about the upcoming tour. We had to move your desk over here, next to mine and Ella's." She pointed to the other desks. "Priya and Ruby sit there, and then we hired Charlotte to help Ella with music publicity, Phoebe for contracts, and Winsome to help me with publishing. We're looking into hiring someone to help Ruby with the TV and media clients."

Rachel went to Julie's desk, situated along the back wall closest to the kitchen. There was her old computer and various office accessories and supplies, for when Julie really got started on her job.

"So as we discussed, this is the start of a brand new branch. There are a lot of tasks at hand. Since we had to go over the timeline with the lawyers, we've included you in the shared Google calendar. You'll be able to see what we need done and by when," Rachel said, leaning against the desk. Purple suede points peeked out from her white trouser pants, her black blouse tucked into the high waist. A vintage plaid blazer with a shimmery purple lining was splayed across the back of her chair. Gold rings glinted on her fingers, earrings poking through her sleek hair.

Julie had always felt inspired by Rachel's class and fashion; she was excited to be back in her orbit and even more hopeful about the knowledge they would impart to the women helped by the nonprofit.

"I'll have to dip once everyone arrives, so it'll just be you and the others. Priya and Ruby are more or less seasoned, but you've been around since the start. I'm deferring to you to be in charge, should the need arise. I know it goes without saying, but obviously, please keep things between you and Ruby professional."

The office door opened, letting in a swarm of laughing women. The sound echoed in through the vaulted ceilings; all five employees arrived at the same time. Julie tried to shake hands and make appropriate eye contact with each one. She didn't want to give anyone a reason to think she was treating Ruby differently than the others.

Ruby came in and, without so much as glancing at Julie, took her seat. She didn't join in the excitement or the greetings. She just sat there, intent on her computer.

Once the others gave their introductions and took their chairs, Julie caught Rachel's eye. She nodded towards Ruby and furrowed her brow. Rachel shrugged.

"Alright, I have to head out. Any issues, please defer to Priya in HR or Julie as acting manager." Rachel waved goodbye and slipped out. Julie sat at her desk, surveying the room. Someone had started the playlist the original three had created for the office, but it was extended with the newcomers' additions. Everyone kept to themselves, focused on papers or their screens,

Not once did Ruby interact with Julie.

She couldn't decide if it was rude or for the better.

45

Anthony paced in the hall outside Gideon's apartment, shaking out his hands. It felt like he was about to go into a boxing ring. He might have better luck with that instead.

Gideon opened the door. "Hey, man. I thought a stampede was coming through here with all that bouncing."

Anthony followed his cousin into the space that was quickly becoming a second home. It was cozy, the walls a cool white except one large accent wall in the living room where they'd used a darker gray. Plants hung from the ceiling and decorated every surface area. Ella's cat, Pollack, meowed at Anthony while he followed him through the rooms. Anthony plopped on the black couch, pulling the fluffy white throw blanket against him. Gideon came out of the kitchen with two bottles of ginger beer. Handing one to Anthony, he sat down and took a sip.

"What's up, Ant? Your text sounded urgent."

Oh, fuck. Where did he start? How could he start?

"It is urgent. I just honestly don't know where to start."

Gideon set his bottle on the stone-topped coffee table and turned to face Anthony. "Well, now I don't give a flying fuck where you start. Is everything okay? Is it your dad?"

Anthony laughed. "Oh, you have no idea." He cleared his throat but not his smile. "Do you remember anything specific from, say, October 2006 to February 2008?"

He watched his cousin scrunch his face up. "Dude, that was so long ago. That was..." Gideon straightened. "Well, October 2006 would've been about a year and half after my dad passed. And February 2008 was a few months before your mom left. Why, what's up with those dates?"

"Do you want me to tell you or do you want to figure it out for yourself?"

Gideon stared at him. Anthony saw how the fear coursed through him, from the way his leg started shaking to his eyes widening ever so slightly. His skin took on a pallid hue.

"Tell me."

Anthony took a deep breath and launched into how he'd stumbled upon his findings. The note, the whiskey, the box. The bible, the necklace, the photographs. And finally, the letters. He watched Gideon's demeanor change, from denial to anger to defeat. The longer Anthony went on, the more Gideon sank into the couch. When he finished, his cousin refused to look at him, his arms crossed over his belly, his knees pushing the coffee table farther away. When Gideon didn't say anything for some time, Anthony reached into his jacket pocket.

"Here."

Bible, necklace, photographs, letters. He placed the items on the couch between them. Gideon picked up the the necklace, fingering the cord around his neck. He pulled it off and held the two necklaces side by side. Anthony couldn't really remember a time when his cousin hadn't worn that necklace, and now he saw why. The two matched. Gideon stared at them for a moment longer before handing Anthony his father's cord.

The photographs were next. Gideon anguished over each photograph, his hands visibly shaking as he came across some of his father and then the portrait of his mother. He stared into her face as Anthony had. Anthony wasn't sure what Gideon was looking for, but Anthony had been trying to find some clue as to who her look of love was directed toward. When Gideon repackaged the photographs in the envelope, he sighed. His shoulders sagged as he looked at the stack of letters.

"How long did it take you to read all of them?"

"All morning. I wanted to take my time. I can leave them with you for a couple days. I just need to put them back before my dad returns. I haven't decided if or when or how to approach him."

Gideon's head snapped to face Anthony. "You can't say anything."

"What are you talking about? I have to talk to him about this."

"Ant, if you talk to him about this it will ruin everything. He'll know you went through his stuff. He'll probably know that I know. He'll probably talk to my mom, and I don't know how that will impact our relationship. Plus, we're about to go on tour. For months. I personally do not want to go on a six month tour with the man who had an affair with my mom, and who knows that I know."

"You do know how selfish that sounds, right?"

Anthony couldn't believe what he was hearing. "My married father had an affair with your widowed mother. You don't want me to talk about how that might have pushed my mom to leave because you don't want to risk a rift with your mom or a six month tour with the man who slept with your mom, who was single at the time? Do you see how much I have to lose with this?"

"Selfish? Are you kidding me, Ant? How is me trying to keep the peace selfish?"

Anthony stared in disbelief at his cousin. "I — I can't do this right now. Read the letters and then we'll talk." He stood and walked out, ignoring Gideon's pleas to come back.

If his dad had an affair the year leading up to his mom leaving, why would his mom completely cut him off?

None of it made sense, but there were three people who could help it make sense. One had run away upstate for a month. One was hiding out in Connecticut with her new family. And one was living a quiet life here in the city. Anthony would have to wait for his dad to return. But until then, he would talk to Gideon about speaking to Amelia.

46

The address scribbled on the paper matched the one on the building in front of her and on the Google Maps screen pulled up on Julie's phone. It was nicer than Julie had imagined, especially for the price point and the location. The agent she was supposed to be meeting wasn't here, and she still wasn't a hundred percent convinced she was at the right apartment.

She was in the heart of the West Village, only a couple blocks south of Washington Square Park. The building was nondescript but clean, with neatly manicure square patches of grass bookending the stoop.

"Hi, you must be Julie."

A young man was walking towards her, his smile

blinding. He held a briefcase in one hand and thrust out his other for a shake before he'd even reached her. She met him halfway, clasping his hand. "You must be Oliver. Rachel told me you owe her for helping you pass college?"

"Yeah, that sounds about right. Couldn't have done it without her." He led her to the building. "Okay, you ready? This is a gem of an apartment, it technically hasn't even come on the market yet. Follow me."

Oliver started climbing the stairs in his snazzy navy suit, not stopping until they reached the fourth floor. Julie tried to catch her breath; she couldn't remember the last time she'd had to climb so many stairs. He opened the door and let her in first.

"I normally let my clients walk around on their own, and then I do a walk through with them in case they have questions. But it's a three bedroom, two bath for $3,500. The building was built in 1910, management is on call. Pets are allowed. Appliances updated a couple of years ago."

Julie thanked Oliver and started making her way around the apartment. The front door opened into the spacious living room that was connected to a relatively small kitchen. One large bedroom and a bathroom stood by the kitchen. On the other side of the living room was a long hallway with a small bedroom Julie could use as an office, the second bathroom, and another large bedroom with a fire escape. She moseyed back to the living room, where Oliver was walking around, hands in his pocket and his head looking around the ceiling.

"This is a really beautiful apartment."

"It is, isn't it?" He beamed like a proud parent. "I really just want it to go to a good person. It's spacious, will it just be you living here?"

Julie blushed. "For now. I'm actually looking into fostering. I have more than enough to give, and I'm tired of my life feeling like it's on pause. I figure I could use one room as an office or play area." She was still getting used to saying it out loud. It was bold, a late twenty-something single woman applying to foster children. It made her belly and her heart fill with butterflies.

"Wow, that's fantastic. This would be a great spot for a family. You're right by Washington Square, the famed West 4th Street basketball courts, seven subway lines are a five to ten minute walk from here."

Julie walked through the apartment once more, Oliver tailing. He looked at her with a newfound gentleness. When they circled back to the living room, Julie knew this was her new home.

"What do you need from me for this to go through? Rachel told be to bring paystubs, checks, bank statements, and copy of a photo ID." Julie pulled the necessary papers from her jacket. She'd hoped this apartment would be The One and wanted to be prepared in case it actually was.

"Well, normally I'd say we'd have to go back to my office to file paperwork. But I'm a bit worried on how fast this one will move, so I brought the paperwork with me. We can fill it out here and I might be able to close it before I even reach the office."

Oliver opened his briefcase, pulling out application papers. He pointed out where to fill in her information and where to sign. He stabled her application with the documents she'd brought, tucking it inside is briefcase.

"Alright, Ms. Milligan. Looks to me I'll be calling you within the next day or two with news of your new apartment." He held out a hand. When she went to shake it, he warmly covered it with his other hand. Oliver grabbed his briefcase, locking the door behind Julie.

She wanted to cry with how happy, how right, her life finally felt.

47

"Anthony?"

He was surprised that Julie picked up the phone after the second ring.

"Hey, Jules." He released a sigh, the shakiness betraying anxiety. "I was wondering if you'd be able to meet today. You know, to talk about things."

"To talk about us, you mean."

"Yeah. I — I'm actually in your neck of the woods, if you're free now?"

He waited through her pause. "Yeah, could you give me a half hour or so? I just got home, I'm working at — at Maven Media."

Anthony scrunched his face. Ah. She still worked with Ruby.

"Of course. See you soon." He hung up and

shoved the phone back in his pocket. He was curious how things had gone between her and Ruby. He hadn't spoken to the feisty red-head since she told him to figure out what he wanted. And, like a moth to a flame, it was Julie.

It'd always be Julie, if he could find a way to trust her with his heart.

He walked around, exploring streets he'd never been down until it was time to meet her. Saying hello to the from desk clerk, Anthony waited for the slow climb of the elevator to drop him at her floor. When he knocked on her door, he could hear her hesitant steps on the other side. It took her minute to open the door to him. It didn't matter how long it took; she stole his breath every time.

She looked up at him, sheepishly, sweeping over his face and body like she was trying to learn it. He knew she could memorize every curve, every scar, if he leaned closer, placed her hands on him.

"Come on in." Julie stepped back into the entry so he could pass through the door. Anthony took off his shoes, watching her pad down the hall in a curve-hugging black dress, blonde waves bouncing the overhead light like a sun.

His sun.

Following after her, he found her leaning against the kitchen sink with her arms crossed.

"Have you eaten yet?" Julie's voice was soft but her eyes said something different, as did her flushed skin.

"No, have you?"

"Nope." She turned to a drawer and pulled out several stacks of take-out menus. He chuckled, remembering how she liked to hoard menus and order the best item from different places to make a meal.

Julie tried to fight a smile, shaking her head at him. "I know what you're thinking, just order something. I'm starving."

"As you wish."

Her smile fell at one of her favorite movie lines, but she didn't say anything. Anthony wanted, needed, to know where she stood with him. Desperate to get the conversation started, he chose Chinese and ordered what had once been their favorite order. When the call had been placed, they stood across from each other. Anthony didn't want to believe there was an awkwardness in the air, but the way she shifted on her feet suggested otherwise.

"Hey, let's go sit down." Anthony held out his hand.

He watched her look at it and bite her lip before snaking her fingers through his. Her palm was small, fitting perfectly in his larger one. Anthony led her to the couch and sat down closer than he had the last time.

"So." Julie's dress rode up to the middle of her creamy thighs, peaches and cream he wanted to lick and bite and worship. He must've been staring; she blushed and adjusted in her seat, tugging the dress down.

"So." It was his turn to blush, and he cleared his throat. "How was work?"

"You mean how was it with Ruby."

Anthony shouldn't have been surprised by her directness. She was a lawyer, but since coming back from her travels, that part of her had almost disappeared. He scratched his head, his fingers tracing his scar.

"Anthony, I need to know what happened. I need to know where you stand."

He met her gaze. Julie wanted him to show her all his cards before showing hers. She'd tried pulling that before, last year, when she'd been tasked to keep an eye on him and his sobriety. But he'd learned his lesson — if he didn't push, she would never give an inch.

"Tit for tat." He crossed his arms. "Like last year."

"Fine. Am I too late?"

Anthony pursed his lips and exhaled. That wasn't the question he'd expected. He thought her questions would have more to do about the woman he was seeing.

"I'm not sure, Julie." He searched her face for something, anything, that would give away what she was thinking. She sat like a stone, unchanging.

"Why did you want to see me?"

"Because I still love you, Anthony. I never stopped. And I want to know if I'm too late."

48

Julie was so tired of being vague and not saying or asking for what she wanted.

He'd asked. She'd answered. All her cards were on the table. She stopped caring if it wasn't enough; she'd find a way to move on if he couldn't find a way to be with her.

"I never stopped loving you either, Julie. But you took off. You won my heart, I trusted you. And then out of nowhere, you just... You said it was a mistake. How am I supposed to move past that?"

"I don't know, Anthony." And she didn't. She looked at this man she'd fought for last year, desperate for him to know his own self-worth and to trust people. This beautiful man with a heart of gold, who saw through her guards and still pushed her to be better. To be herself.

"What I do know is that I am sorry I led you on and I'm sorry I ended things — I know that letting you go was the biggest mistake I'd made. That there would be a chance you wouldn't come back. But I'm most certainly not sorry for coming back as someone who knows what they want and who finally, *finally* loves themself. I'm not sorry for figuring out who am I. And I'm not sorry for healing myself. I love you, and I understand if you've moved on. If you can't trust me. But know that I know who I am, I know what I want, and while I promise I will never push you away like that again, I also promise I will continue to grow and change and try and be the best version of myself. I will bring that to our relationship every day. I just... I don't want to lose you again, Anthony."

Julie caught her breath. She hadn't planned on completely spilling her guts to him. But feeling the way he saw and listened to her, she couldn't stop herself. She needed him to know she was all in, for good.

Anthony only stared at her, his expression unchanging. He finally leaned back and stretched his arms above him, a hand going to his head. She waited for what seemed like an eternity for him to say something.

"I want to be with you, Julie. I want to put everything behind us and move forward. I believed you when you said how you felt. But it is a matter of trust, and that takes time." He turned toward her, taking her hands in his. "I am willing to work on that trust so long as I can be with you. For real. All in. We did the casual dating. We did the friends getting to know each other. We did the time apart, see other people thing. But what all of that has taught me is that, at the end of the day, I just want you. I want to pick up where we left off. I want to continue getting to know you, loving you, while we rebuild that trust."

He brought her hands to his lips, decorating each finger with a kiss before turning her hands over and doing the same to her palms. Instinctively, Julie cupped his face. She felt the way his jaw rippled against her skin, the way he fought to find new ground to lay his claim. He worked his way down her arms as her fingers ran through his hair, stopping above the steep ridge of his scar, a reminder of one of many obstacles they'd overcome. He was strong, a mountain that could not be torn down. But the strength of this man lay in his vulnerability, his ability to change. To accept, to love, and to forgive.

Julie slid her hands back along his neck, pulling his face up from the skin he brushed with his mouth. Felt her body respond to his affections. She met his luminous eyes and fell into them, knowing he would catch her. She could spend forever staring into those depths. Anthony's hands found their way to her face, their coarseness heavy against her skin as he cupped her face. They didn't need words. The way his fingers gripped the back of her neck, his thumbs finding her cheek, giving her access to the intimate nature of loving someone's hands.

He was hers as much as she was his.

49

Anthony held living fire in his hands, the heat from Julie's skin threatening to burn if he didn't become one with her. He leaned his forehead against hers, breath mingling, warm, lips too far away. Closing the distance, he needed to consume and be consumed, to drink from one another, two lost souls finding their other.

The plunge of her tongue sent a shock of desire to his center. The plea for more became a demand when Julie pushed against him, a soft moan escaping. Anthony's hard length pressed against the denim constraints of his pants and he pushed back, sending Julie on her back beneath him. Her legs parted to embrace his hips as he settled between her, hands tangling in the soft curls of her hair. Vanilla and rose.

Home.

Julie's fingers outlined the ridges of his shoulders blades, gliding their way along the divot of his spine and to the hem of his shirt, dancing on the fevered skin beneath. The jolt of her cool skin sent his body closer to hers, desperate for refuge in her heat. His lips nipped and licked the column of her neck until her hips were raising, grinding, crashing against his, her hands between his skin and shirt. She gripped his body with every part of hers, begging for more.

Anthony trailed kisses from her neck to the line between her chest, anxious to free her curves from her dress. Panting, he rose onto his knees, Julie's hands falling to his waistband. She curled her fingers in his belt loops, anxious to have him closer. He stayed kneeling, memorizing the flush of her cheeks surrounded by gold. Relearning the curves of her arms as they reached for him, the curves of her legs as they held him. The dress was hiked around her hips; he needed the feel of her lush thighs in his hands to stay forever imprinted in his brain.

"Anthony, I need you." Her voice was low, sultry, heavy with truth.

He leaned forward, over her, unable to deny the need matched by the fear.

What if this was all a dream?

"I need you. I needed you before, and I'll need you every time after this one. I just can't go through last time again."

Her hands slid down to his thighs and squeezed. "I know. Let me show you it won't be like last time. Trust me."

Those two words had always presented a wall to Anthony. Faced with them once again by the woman he loved, he felt himself push back. He knew if they were ever going to love the way they deserved, the wall would need to come down. Anthony wanted a lifetime of these moments with Julie, and he wanted the rest of his life to start right now.

"Show me." He lifted off the couch, holding out his hands to help her up. She led them to her bedroom, closing the door behind them and turning her back to him.

"Unzip me."

Anthony stood behind her. Pushing her hair to one side, he gripped the tiny zipper between his fingers, leaving languid kisses on her neck while he exposed her back. Her head fell against his shoulders, back arching to push herself closer to him.

Anthony slid his hands into the new opening of the dress, her skin burning while he explored. Her back gave way to wide hips, and he trailed his fingers along her soft belly to her breasts, cupping them, teasing the nipples through her lacy bra. She moaned his name, leaning against him as her hands searched for his member.

He released her, moving his hands along her upper back. Slowly peeling the split sides of the dress from her body. Julie let the garment fall to the floor in a heap, giving a generous view of her ample backside. His hands pulled her hips against him, his cock pressed between the heart-shaped cheeks of her ass. Anthony splayed one hand on her stomach, the other unclipping her bra. The lacy plum lingerie slid down Julie's arms. Once free, she spun to face him.

Her fingers played with the hem of his shirt, and he raised his arms. She slid the fabric over his head, littering kisses along his chest, his torso, nipping at his pecs and abs, filling the valleys with licks. Dropping to her knees, Julie undid his pants, guiding them down his legs. His cock strained against his cotton underwear, threatening to break now that he was free from the thicker prison of his jeans. He shimmied out, kicking them to the side, and almost collapsed from weak knees. Julie massaged his thickness while she teased the twin orbs beneath.

Julie gripped his thighs and lapped at the tip of his cock, swirling her tongue along the head. Licking the length of him, she brought her mouth to his balls, sucking on one and then the other. He was fighting gravity, the way she moaned and worked his shaft, the tandem of her mouth licking and hand pressing himself deep inside her mouth.

"Wait." He nearly gasped, placing a hand on the back of her head, slowing her rocking. This was something he'd held onto, dreamt of, for months; if they didn't stop, he'd finish too soon. And the fun hadn't even started.

She slowed, easing him from her mouth with a flick of that talented tongue. As she rose, Anthony bent and picked her up, throwing her legs around his hips so he was nestled by her wet core. He carried her the couple steps to the bed, laying his goddess on crisp sheets he couldn't wait to mess up.

50

Julie looked up at Anthony hovering above her, the sculpt of his dense biceps on either side of her head reflecting the low light in her bedroom. Her hands reveled in the cut of his abs, the corded muscle of his back. She felt the beauty of his body, strong, loving, hers. Arched her back to bring herself closer to what she'd been missing. Anthony took her mouth in his, and she tasted ginger and citrus. Lust and love.

She'd never been good about staying away.

"I need you." Her breath was husky, laden with him.

"I've always needed you." His eyes burned with desire as he placed a gentle kiss in the middle of her forehead. "You're so beautiful."

She tilted her head to meet his, needing to taste

him once more. Needing to lose herself in this love she believed in. The way his hands and mouth explored every in of her body, inside and out, set her body on fire.

"Do you have a condom?" She whispered against his mouth, her hand finding his thick shaft poised between her legs. He was heavy with desire, brushing along the soft underside of her belly, gasoline to the flames inside her.

Anthony bent to the floor and rose with a condom. Julie took it from him, rolling it down his engorged shaft. His fingers tested the hot folds of her sex.

"And you're wet," he groaned, taking the slick digits in his mouth. He sucked and licked, placing a wet finger on her clit. The touch sent a surge of desire rolling through her, and she bucked her hips.

He placed himself at her entrance, holding her gaze as he eased himself into her wet heat. Julie cried out, the exquisite size of him stretching her walls, the touch of his finger against her sensitive bud ready to send her flying. Her breath stuttered as he found an excruciatingly slow rhythm with his hips, gradually speaking until it matched the beat of her heart, the pulse between her legs. His length pressed into her harder, and her body responded, demanding more. There'd been an empty space inside her body and her heart for too long, spaces only he could fill. Sweat rolled from his defined muscles, her breasts pressed against his godly chest, the insistent demand of his cock inside her begging for release.

Julie surrendered to the god above as he worshipped her most sacred space with his own, claiming her as she did him. He filled her temple, her name a chant on his lips. Her body trembled with release, his and hers, their cries merging into one. He collapsed above her, panting, bodies sliding from sweat pooled between them. Julie clutched him to her, desperate to believe this was real. If she let go, she might wake and find it had all been a dream.

Anthony rolled off her and pulled her into his chest. Julie felt the rise and fall of his chest, kissing the place where his heart beat. Where her heart belonged. She wasn't sure how long they laid there, it would never be enough. Anthony stirred in her arms. His fingers slid gently along her spine, from the base of her neck to the top of her crease.

"I'm completely in love with you, Juliette. I'm all yours." His lips found hers, a gentle badge to mark the truth in his words. "Forever and always."

51

Anthony cracked his eyes, the room awash in the gray-blue of early morning. There was the smell of vanilla, rose that had haunted him every moment of the last few months. And when he saw the crazed blonde hair splayed across his chest, he was tempted to pinch himself. The sleeping form stirred, a heavy hand pushing the hair aside to reveal the love of his life.

His dream had become his reality.

Smiling, he brushed a kiss on the top of her head. "Good morning, sunshine."

The words brought him back to a time last year when a perfect night had been upended the next morning. And it had started very similarly to this. When Julie didn't respond, Anthony closed his eyes, fighting the rising panic. Had he really been a fool to fall for this again?

Her hand scaled his torso and rested on his neck. Kisses drifted along his chest, his nipple pinched and then soothed by the warm flick of a tongue.

"Good morning, handsome."

Anthony dared himself to open his eyes. Julie rested her chin between his pecs, a lazy smile hardly seen through her cloud of hair. He released a sigh of relief, trying to calm his pounding heart from bursting through his chest. Julie chuckled, a hand pressed against the very spot he was trying to calm.

"Damn, are you okay? It's like a horse race in there."

"Yep. Yeah. Peachy. How are you?"

Julie rolled back over and nestled into his side. "Perfect. I love you forever."

Hearing those words from her mouth while she was curled into him — naked — was all he'd need for the rest of his life.

"Forever?"

She laughed. "Forever. I promise."

Thanks so much for reading! Continue Anthony and

Julie's story with MORE THAN WE LOVED. Julie wins back Anthony's trust, and their relationship is finally on steady ground, but tense family issues threaten to come between them — and a decision Julie made will change their lives forever.

More Than We Loved is available wherever books are sold.

LINKS

Did you enjoy this book? Leave a review and let others know!

Find me online:

Facebook
Instagram
Website

Printed in Great Britain
by Amazon